SLOW BURN

A FUREVER VETERINARY ROMANCE

CARA MALONE

LISBON PRESS

Copyright © 2022 by Cara Malone

All rights reserved.

No part of this book may be reproduced in any form or by any electronic or mechanical means, including information storage and retrieval systems, without written permission from the author, except for the use of brief quotations in a book review.

1
LAUREN

"And you have the budget ready for me to review, right?" Gary asked.

Lauren barely heard the question, but it did register as an annoying buzz in the back of her mind. She was juggling her demanding boss, a new resident intake, and a mischievous resident who was *literally* juggling mini muffins from the breakfast buffet.

Besides, she'd already sent Gary her budget *and* he approved it via email last week. He just wanted to feel like he was doing something boss-ish while he was here.

"Yes," she humored him. "We can review it in my office after Angelique goes over the nurses' station protocols with you."

"What's that now?" Angelique, who was just innocently passing them in the hall, looked like she'd been sideswiped by a bus, and Lauren made a mental note to apologize for it later.

"Remember, you volunteered to show Mr. Peterson how you chart?" she fibbed.

God bless Angelique, she was one of the best nurses on staff and also had the most seniority in the building. She registered Lauren's distress and jumped right into the fray. "Oh yes, right this way, Mr. Peterson."

Lauren mouthed *thank you* as soon as Gary turned his back to her and Angelique stuck her tongue out in return. She was a pro at her job, with sass to match – one of the reasons why she was so beloved by the residents here at the Sunnyside Senior Living Community.

Lauren Carpenter was the facility director, had been for about nine months now, and Gary was here doing his quarterly checking up on her, make sure she was running the Granville location according to corporate's exacting standards.

Which, speaking of... a mini muffin rolling across the floor and hitting the toe of her shoe reminded Lauren that there were still fires to be put out. Why did the place have to go nuclear on the one day her boss traveled in from Cleveland?

"Opal, honey, do you think you could find something better to juggle than baked goods?" she asked as she tossed the muffin at her feet into a nearby trash can.

"Why? People love it!" her most challenging resident shot back at her, not missing a beat in picking up a replacement muffin from the basket.

Opal was nearly a hundred years old, with more mischief in her than a four-and-a-half-foot-tall silver-haired woman ought to be able to contain. Lauren had never seen her sick or even lacking her signature wicked grin, and she had to grudgingly admit that Opal had a particular talent for drawing out the more introverted residents. When she wasn't juggling mini muffins, Opal was known to act out whole episodes of *The Andy Griffith Show* to cheer people up or go from suite to suite handing out dirty literature to those so inclined.

Still... today of all days?

"Opal, please," Lauren sighed, just as the caregiver assigned to breakfast duty emerged from the kitchen with a chafing dish of scrambled eggs.

He scanned the room, immediately zeroing in on the problem even as Opal tried to play innocent and set the muffins down on her plate. "I'm so sorry, Lauren, I just stepped away for a fresh batch of eggs."

"It's no problem, Miguel, you got it from here?" she asked. "Mr. Peterson is here today and I need to catch up with him."

He nodded, catching the meaning behind her words. *Now is not the time for Opal's shenanigans.* "Got it, boss."

Lauren took a deep breath, blowing dark brown tendrils out of her face on the exhale. Did she look as frazzled as she felt? Impossible to know, and it wasn't like she'd have the chance to glance in a mirror anytime soon.

Most of the time, she felt in control here. She felt like she was doing a good job and her residents *and* her employees were happy – no easy feat, accomplished with no small amount of compromises. That didn't make her immune to panic when Gary's hot, acrid breath started warming her neck, though.

In a perfect world, *elder care* and *corporate* were words that would never be spoken in the same sentence. Everyone would get the care and attention they needed without talk of budgets and overhead and profits. Hell, in a perfect world, no one would care about Opal and her juggling antics as long as she was happy.

In this world, though, men like Gary Peterson existed, and they lived to scrutinize. To trim the budgetary fat. To enforce inflexible corporate policies.

He certainly wasn't amused to walk in this morning and learn what breakfast entertainment was on offer. Lauren could just see it in his eyes – every dropped mini muffin an unnecessary waste, a direct blow to the facility's budget. Probably what got him antsy to review it all over again.

The sooner Lauren could get him out the door and back to Cleveland for another three months, the better.

But Angelique would have to keep him busy just a little longer, because there was one more fire to put out this morning. It was the new resident moving into suite number seventeen, and her very high-strung family.

"Don't forget to breathe," Opal called from the dining room as Lauren turned away. "You're a boss bitch!"

Lauren couldn't help smiling. While *bitch* was a word she could do without hearing screamed down the hall on this particular morning, it did amuse her every time it came out of Opal's mouth. The secret to being feisty and happy into your late nineties? Apparently, it was staying current with pop culture and adopting the slang whenever it suited you.

"Thank you, Opal," she waved over her shoulder. Then she made her way to the residential wing.

Sunnyside had a variety of living arrangements available, from fully-equipped independent living suites to hospice rooms, and about a hundred total residents. The newest arrival, Rose Moreno, fell in the middle of the spectrum – she'd been diagnosed with ovarian cancer almost a decade ago and after multiple unsuccessful attempts at treatment, she'd now chosen palliative care. She was eighty-one years old, here to be made comfortable by the nurses, and to lighten the burden on her family, who weren't up to the challenges of at-home nursing.

That was a pretty common scenario, and nothing about it had surprised Lauren when she met Rose during her initial tour of the facility.

What was waiting for her in suite seventeen, on the other hand... Could nothing go well today? Would that be too much to ask?

"We were told she would have a lake view!" Rose's adult daughter was practically screeching at the caregiver helping Rose move in her things. "Does this look like a lake view?!"

"Really, Gina, it doesn't bother me," Rose was saying from the recliner that had already been moved in. "The view is fine."

"Fine? It's an ugly parking lot!" Gina huffed.

Lauren knocked on the doorframe to announce herself, and took advantage of the momentary chaos to glance out the window herself. None of the rooms had a parking lot view for privacy reasons, but if one were to stand right next to the window like Gina was doing and really crane one's head, it would be possible to see a small corner of pavement.

"Can we help you?" Gina barked.

"I'm Lauren Carpenter," she said. "Facility director. We met during the tour, and I just wanted to stop in to say hi and–" *Diffuse a bomb,* she thought.

"Change my mother's room assignment, I hope!" Gina said, hands on hips. "Where is the lake?"

"Gina, stop," a man said from the corner. He was about Gina's age, and Lauren hadn't even noticed him there. He nodded toward Lauren now. "I'm Mike, Rose's son." He avoided looking Gina's way, as if he didn't even want to take ownership of his sister in this moment. "The suite is nice."

"Yes, it's perfectly fine," Rose said. "I'm sure the lake view was an innocent oversight, and honestly, I don't need it–"

"Mom, this is going to be your room for the rest of your–" Gina's voice cracked and instead of finishing her sentence, she whirled on Lauren. "Are you going to fix this or what?"

She'd dealt with the likes of Gina plenty of times before. It hadn't taken much time on the job before she'd learned to spot the various ways that people displayed and dealt with their grief. Gina, apparently, woke up today and chose anger.

"Ms... may I call you Gina?" she asked, already

approaching her with an outstretched hand. "Please, have a seat."

"Ms. Moreno," she said, reluctantly letting Lauren sit her down in a chair at a small dining table along the wall.

"Ms. Moreno, please just sit back and relax while we take care of bringing in the rest of your mother's belongings," Lauren said, nodding in the caregiver's direction. He took his cue, and Mike also took the opportunity to bug out. They both disappeared down the hall, and Lauren turned back to Gina and Rose. "Can I get either of you anything? Coffee, water, a mini muffin?"

There might still be one stuck to my heel, she thought, then brushed aside her irritation. If Gina's mood rubbed off on her, Gina won.

"I'm fine, thank you, dear," Rose said. She was dwarfed by the plush recliner she was sitting in, her pure white hair lying wavy over her shoulders. There were deep laugh lines and crow's feet carved into the contours of her face, signs of a life well lived, and she was smiling even now.

"Yeah, it's fine," Gina said, her tone implying it was anything but.

Time to mend some fences, now that she wasn't actively yelling. Lauren stepped over to the window, pointing to some tall ornamental grasses about ten yards away. "I apologize for any confusion," she said, "but there is a lake on the other side of that grass. The landscaping crew leaves it long in the spring because there are sparrows who like to nest in it, but the lake will be visible in a few months."

"Oh, sparrows, that sounds lovely!" Rose said, and Lauren watched Gina's face as her expression slowly morphed from indignant to mildly embarrassed. Maybe it was wrong to find pleasure in someone else's discomfort, but after the way their conversation started off, it was satisfying to watch her realize her own unreasonableness.

"Well, someone could have explained that," was all Gina managed, not looking Lauren in the eye.

"We'll get you all moved in, Rose, and in the afternoon we've got a string quartet coming in if you'd like to attend," she went on, as if the whole ordeal hadn't happened. "They're students from the local university and they like to have a live audience to practice for before their senior showcase, so they come in about once per semester."

"That would be nice," Rose said. "Can't say I've ever heard a string quartet live before."

"I'll make sure someone comes to get you before the performance," Lauren promised. Then she got the heck out of the room before Gina could find anything else to bitch about. True, she was just trying to process her mother's illness – and the fact of her mortality – but that didn't mean Lauren had to sign up for another round of verbal abuse.

Hopefully, neither would any of her staff.

She was breathing a little easier on her way back up the hallway. Three fires fought and extinguished in under an hour? Not bad. And as long as she humored Gary with some favorable budget numbers, he'd leave happy today too.

She went to the nurses' station to relieve Angelique of her burden, and her breath caught in her throat once more as her eyes locked with a drop-dead gorgeous woman with a... *fox?* On her shoulder?

Either this day just threw one more surprise at Lauren, or she needed to have her head checked.

2

GRACE

"Ah, here's the director now," the nurse said, looking a little relieved not to have to deal with Grace and her fox.

She turned, and the professional *sorry to drop in like this* smile she wore instantly turned into more of a drool as she took in the unexpectedly young, beautiful director. Soft brunette curls fell to chin-length, framing a heart-shaped face and dark, soulful eyes. She was a little shorter than Grace, and a little curvier too. Shapely calves peeked out from under a knee-length black skirt, and her peach-colored lips curled into a wry smile.

"I'm sorry, I don't recall scheduling a... what is that, exactly?"

She was looking at Sonic, perched politely on Grace's shoulder, and her brow furrowed adorably as she tried to puzzle it out.

"You didn't," Grace explained. "This is Sonic, he's a fennec fox." She extended her hand. "And my name is

Grace Williams. I'm an animal-assisted therapy provider."

The director's wry smile was bewitching. She asked, "What kind of therapy does Sonic need?"

Grace smiled. "Animal-*assisted* therapy – Sonic's not a patient, he's one of my therapy animals." Well, he was on loan from a friend, but Grace narrowly avoided blurting out all those unnecessary details. She'd practiced her pitch at home and in front of her vet friends dozens of times, but in real life, in front of such a gorgeous woman, it was proving much more difficult to control the urge to over-explain. "I'm expanding my practice into this region–" Starting, more like. "–and I'd love just a few minutes of your time to explain how Sonic and I can help your residents."

The director frowned. "I'm very busy today."

Grace reached for the satchel slung over her shoulder, trying to extract the pamphlets she'd printed off just last week. Gathering mountains of statistics on the benefits of animal-assisted therapy for elderly populations had been part of her master's thesis, and assembling them into attractive, digestible literature had been the first official step in opening her practice.

When she was slaving over the computer, wondering if she should just hire a graphic designer, she'd thought that was the hard part.

Turns out, keeping her mouth from running away from her in front of a potential client was the real hard work.

"Here, I have–"

She pulled a small stack of pamphlets out of the satchel, accidentally bringing a dried cherry out of the bag with them. Sonic's ears pinged straight up as he caught the smell, and he vaulted down Grace's arm, using her hand as a springboard and nimbly snatching the snack.

"Sonic!"

The director yelped with surprise as the small tan fox landed in her arms. Grace opened her mouth to apologize profusely, but paused when she noticed the look of pure joy on the woman's face.

"Oh my gosh, he's so soft!"

"Still learning personal boundaries, too," Grace said, holding her hands out, but the woman didn't pass him back. Instead, she stroked between his ears. All her objections about being busy melted away, and she seemed entirely lost in the moment.

Grace set her pamphlets down on the counter, seizing the only opportunity she was likely to get to make her pitch. The script she'd prepared felt stiff and impersonal now, so she threw it out and decided to follow Sonic's lead – she'd simply take a leap of faith.

"How do you feel right now?" she asked the director. "Calm? Present? Happy?"

The woman looked up, her milk-chocolate eyes dancing with an obvious answer. "All of the above."

"Animals have a powerful effect on people," Grace said. "It only takes a few minutes with one to relax us, lift our spirits, remind us to live in the moment the way they do. That's why they make wonderful companions for people dealing with a variety of mental health issues, and they've also been very effective in raising morale and rejuvenating the elderly." She paused. "I'm sorry, I haven't gotten your name yet."

"Lauren. Carpenter," she said, then reluctantly held Sonic out for Grace. "And all of that sounds wonderful, but I just don't think Sunnyside can handle the added chaos of a fox running around. We have a hard enough time controlling our feistier residents."

She said it with a chuckle, but Grace could tell she was losing her.

"Lauren..." It was a common name, but it had never felt so velvety on Grace's tongue. God, there was something about her, something that made Grace lose her train of thought entirely too often. "I won't take up any more of your time today, but will you please read these pamphlets when you have a moment? It doesn't have to be Sonic – a lot of assisted living facilities see great improvements in their residents with cats or even just a fish tank."

"That does sound more manageable–" Lauren started to say, reaching for the literature on the counter.

"What the hell is that?" a male voice boomed, making both Lauren and Sonic flinch. Grace looked over the director's shoulder to see a balding man in a cheap suit coming up the hall toward them.

"A fennec fox," Lauren said, turning to him. "Mr. Peterson, I was just coming to find you. This is Grace Williams. She runs a therapy animal program and she says–"

"No," the man said, his face scrunching up meanly. "No animals – can you imagine the liability issues?"

"Actually–" Grace started, but he cut her off.

"Please get that thing out of here before it gives one of our residents Lyme disease," he said. Then he turned his back on Grace, clearly done with her. "Lauren, are you ready to go over the quarterly budget?"

"Sure, Mr. Peterson," Lauren said, her smile gone, her voice tired.

"Fennecs aren't carriers for Lyme–" Grace tried one more time, but the man was already leading Lauren away. The director looked over her shoulder at Grace, mouthing the word *sorry* as she left.

Grace glanced at the pamphlets still sitting on the counter, then at the nurse who'd been valiantly attempting to be invisible ever since the bald man showed up.

"Sorry," she said. "Mr. Peterson's a bit of a stickler for the rules."

"Who is he?" Grace asked. "I thought Ms. Carpenter was in charge of this facility."

"She is," the nurse said. "He's the regional manager – from corporate."

"Ah. So, I just hit a brick wall, huh?"

The nurse gave her a sympathetic look. "'Fraid so."

"Damn." Grace had only been in business for a month, and she had a handful of clients who hired her to bring animals in for one-off programs. Bunny yoga. Story time with animals at the library. An after-school program pairing up kids on the autism spectrum with the local humane society for volunteer work. Things like that. But to make inroads with an assisted living facility – especially one like Sunnyside, with multiple locations all over the state – would really mean helping a lot of people.

People like her own father, who really could have used a companion in his final days.

She let out a sigh, then pulled a business card from her bag. "Could you make sure Lauren gets these pamphlets, and my business card, just in case Mr. Peterson has a change of heart?"

"I will," the nurse said, then asked shyly, "if you let me feed Sonic a cherry before you go?"

Grace laughed, then reached into her satchel again. "He'd love that."

3
DEE

Sandra Caldwell woke up with one hell of a pain in her hip. It radiated all the way down her right side, and although it was a pain she experienced every morning, it wasn't one she was capable of getting used to.

Little aches, like the arthritis in her knuckles or the occasional ache in her back, were things you adjusted to. The toll you paid to stay on this earth after a while.

Sandra, who everyone had called Dee for as long as she could remember, was eighty-two years old and all things considered, she was lucky that the searing pain on her right side was the first major problem she'd encountered in this whole ugly business of aging.

She'd fallen out of her bed four months ago. It was only a two-foot drop onto carpet, but after eight decades on this earth, she had a lot less padding than she used to, and her bones were more delicate than they once were. The result was a hairline fracture. She'd been lucky it wasn't a full break, but it still hurt like hell and the recovery period was turning out to be longer than she'd hoped.

Once upon a time, a fall like that wouldn't even have been worth mentioning.

Now, she slowly stretched out her leg, doing some hip rolls for flexibility that the physical therapist had showed her. They worked some of the stiffness out, but what she really needed was to get up and get moving. Unfortunately, that was more of an ordeal these days than it used to be, too.

An hour later, she was showered, dressed, and slowly making her way down the hall toward the dining room. She favored her right leg as she walked and she used a cane now, but she passed several suites where the residents inside were bed-bound, and that helped her remember that things could always be worse.

Eighty-two years old with an aching hip, but at least she was on her feet. Following her nose to the aroma of freshly brewed coffee and mouth-watering bacon. Enough money in her bank account to afford one of the good assisted living facilities, where they don't just dump you in your room and forget about you. Yeah, she was doing alright.

"Hey, Sandra Dee!" a cheerful voice rang out, and Dee's mood darkened.

"Opal," she said, nodding in the older woman's direction.

"Smile, you're above ground!" Opal said. "The muffins are good today too."

They *did* smell good – the scent of blueberries permeated the dining room – but Dee couldn't help her bad mood. Her jaw automatically set itself in a scowl whenever she heard Opal's voice. The woman was forever causing some trouble or another, making extra work for the staff, and it didn't help that it was her grating voice that Dee had heard moments before her accident.

Sandra Dee! Get up, there's a bear outside your window!

She'd startled, fallen, and as the pain shot through her body, so sharp it reached her cheeks, she'd been faintly aware of Opal standing in her doorway, saying, *Oh gosh, it was just a raccoon.*

"Can't believe you're still with us, Opal," Dee said now with a forced smile. "What are you, immortal?"

"One can only hope," Opal answered. "You coming to my hundredth birthday party in a couple months?"

"Wouldn't miss it," Dee said, her jaw refusing to relax as she went over to the row of chafing dishes where the bacon and eggs were being kept warm.

The trick to dealing with Opal was to humor her – but not too much. Dee would make herself a plate, then make up an excuse to go back to her rooms to eat. Or maybe she'd go out on the patio and enjoy the morning sunshine, if it wasn't too cold. She sure as hell wasn't going to sit at the old woman's table and let her badger her into indigestion.

"I'm going to request a bounce house," Opal said while Dee scooped herself some scrambled eggs. "A centenarian ought to be able to make whatever birthday requests she wants, right?"

Dee snorted. "Just don't expect me to get in it with you – bum hip, remember?"

"Oh, are you still mad about that?" Opal tsked. "I've apologized a thousand times."

Dee rolled her eyes, though her back was to Opal so it went unnoticed. In fact, she had *never* apologized. Dee was sure that Opal believed she had, but she'd never actually said the words *I'm sorry*.

"Well, I'm going to get some fresh air," she said, carefully balancing her plate in one hand as she headed for the door.

"Enjoy your day, Sandra Dee."

"You too, Opal," she answered. *Hope I don't see you again until dinner.*

It was chilly on the patio, but peaceful. A lot of the residents didn't have much tolerance for temperature extremes, but Dee had spent her whole life outside and a little cold never bothered her. In her prime she'd been an environmental scientist and she spent a lot of her time out in the field, collecting samples and observing a variety of climates. She'd even been to Antarctica – the patio had nothing on *that* cold.

She ate, then sat sipping her coffee for a long while, watching as sparrows flitted in and out of the tall grasses by the lake. They were building their nests, taking scouting trips and coming back with beaks full of dried grass to prepare for their young.

It was always bittersweet, watching nature take its course like that.

Dee had a younger sister she loved dearly, and a grown niece and nephew who visited when they weren't too busy living their own lives. She had a lot of good friends – although she'd been to more funerals than she cared for at this point in her life.

But she never settled down. Never started a family, which seemed to come so naturally to the sparrows in the tall grass, going about their business without a care in the world.

Partly, it was the world she grew up in. She knew from a very young age that she was different from the 'boy crazy' girls she knew when she was a kid. Her eyes had gone to the fairer sex, along with her heart and every other part of her. She'd lived through the LGBTQ+ rights movement, along with the fight for civil rights and women's rights. She'd seen how long progress really takes, and that nothing is truly fixed just because a couple of laws are enacted, as necessary and overdue as they are.

Dee's niece had come out a few years ago – claiming for herself a label that didn't even exist when Dee was growing up, calling herself pansexual. And while love was never a simple thing, it would be so much easier for her than it was for Dee.

A good thing, a thing that made a happy little lump form in Dee's throat whenever she thought about it.

But the constraints of society weren't the only things that kept Dee from making a family of her own. She'd dated plenty of women, loved a handful of them. But she'd never been head-over-heels, can't-breathe, can't-even-think-when-you're-around *in love* with any of them.

Except for one.

It was so long ago she shouldn't even be able to remember it now. And it had been brief, never had the chance to get off the ground. After, she'd decided that she would never settle for anything less than the all-consuming passion she felt for that woman.

And, as luck or life would have it, every lover she'd ever taken afterward had turned out to be *less.* None of them measured up.

Or maybe you're just a fool who could never tell the difference between puppy love and the mature kind, she'd chided herself plenty of times over the years. It did not escape her, sitting out here on the chilly patio all by herself, that settling down with any one of the women she'd loved over the years would have meant having a companion to grow old with. Someone to keep her company and watch sparrows with and complain about Opal to.

Maybe settling wasn't the worst thing you could do.

When her coffee went cold and her hip started to stiffen again, Dee hauled herself up from her chair and went back inside. She spent the rest of the morning as she usually did – making a couple laps around the halls to keep herself nimble. Saying hello to the nurses, caregivers and residents as she passed them. Stopping in to one of her bedridden friends' suite for a leisurely game of chess. Snacking more than she should from the plentiful treats the staff kept on hand.

She was sitting in the sunroom with another friend, reading aloud from a romance novel on Cora's tablet and thinking it could use more lesbians, when her favorite nurse, Angelique, popped her head in the door.

"Lunchtime, ladies," she said. "Want me to bring you, Cora?"

"I've got her," Dee volunteered. Cora was in a wheelchair, and Dee's motives were not entirely pure – her physical therapist really wanted her to switch from her cane to a walker, but Dee was too proud for that. Pushing Cora's chair would achieve the same thing without bruising her ego. "What's for lunch?"

"Tomato soup and grilled cheese," Angelique said, and Dee's mouth gave a Pavlovian response.

"Make sure Opal doesn't hog it all," Cora said. "This one's a slow walker."

"Not my fault," Dee shot back, setting the tablet in Cora's lap. They'd stopped just before a rather raunchy scene, and she knew Cora would want her to keep reading after lunch. But her vision was bad, so she was at the mercy of either Dee or an audiobook narrator – everyone had their vices, and romance novels were Cora's.

Dee unlocked the brakes on Cora's chair and they made their way across the building to the dining room. Cora was right, Dee moved slow, but what did she want for an eighty-two-year-old? Skid marks in the hallways?

They were about halfway to the dining room when they came to a doorframe decorated in crepe paper flowers – decorating the doors of new residents was a tradition the staff had instituted to help them feel welcome and encourage everyone to introduce themselves.

"Forgot we had a newbie," Dee said. Lauren, the director, had made an announcement about that a week ago, but nobody's memory around here was watertight anymore.

"Oh yeah, a woman, I believe," Cora said. "Should we stop and say hi?"

The door was open and Dee was about to agree, but then she heard bickering coming from inside the suite.

"I told you we should have brought some of her kitchen things!" a woman's voice snapped, sharp and irritable.

"Why would she cook?" a man retorted. "We're paying out the nose for her to have three meals and two snacks a day provided for her."

"But there's a kitchenette!" the woman shot back. "What if she wants a midnight snack?"

"Then she'll use the call button to ask someone to bring her one!"

They both sounded like they were at the end of their rope, and Dee had every intention to breeze right past the open doorway. Unfortunately, the moment she stepped in front of it, her eyes locked on the new resident inside, and Dee froze.

The white-haired woman sat in a recliner in the center of the room, positively dwarfed by the furniture. Their eyes locked, and instead of looking away like two strangers accidentally making eye contact usually did, their gaze lingered. Those pale blue eyes. That upturned nose. Sixty years had taken their toll on the woman's delicate features, but Dee recognized her immediately.

Rose Dennison.

The bewitching herpetologist that stole Dee's heart in the Galapagos during her first research job after grad school.

The one that got away... or that was how she thought of her over the years when she was lying lonely in her bed.

Here at Sunnyside?

Dee glanced at the name plate outside the door, decorated with crepe paper flowers like the rest of it. *Rose Moreno.* She must have gotten married, but unless Dee had completely lost her marbles, this was the same woman – and a miracle had just occurred.

"Hello?" Rose said, and Dee's heart leaped into her throat.

Before she could formulate a response, the shrill younger woman looked at Dee and her eyes widened in surprise. Then she marched over and swung the door shut.

Dee looked at Cora, whose eyes were wide too.

"Nice family," she huffed.

"Yeah, guess we're not introducing ourselves after all," Dee said, feeling breathless as she continued on toward the dining room. By the time they arrived, the whole incident was starting to feel like a dream and she wondered if she'd had a momentary bout of dementia. If she had, it would be her first – her body might be breaking down, but her mind had always been a steel trap.

But Rose Dennison was the lost love she'd held onto for six decades.

And she was here? That wasn't possible, was it?

4
ROSE

1964

Rose Dennison stepped off the ferry and onto solid ground, the movement feeling monumental as well as a little unsteady. She'd been traveling for almost a full day, and even though she'd been exhausted by the time she got on the ferry, her whole body was buzzing with excitement now.

The island air was warm, with that uniquely coastal smell on the breeze. Not far from the dock, the greenery took over, and walking with the rest of her team, Rose felt like she was stepping into a jungle. A jungle with cacti growing up right next to the trees.

She was on Santa Cruz Island in the center of the Galapagos, on her way to the newly opened Charles Darwin Research Station. When the opportunity arose, via a graduate school professor who saw her potential, Rose felt like the luckiest girl in the world. Now that she was actually here, slapping at mosquitos and sweating already, she knew this was a dream come true.

The staff member who'd come to greet the scientists at the dock led them to a Land Rover, and they all piled in.

"How soon can I see the tortoises?" Rose asked from the back seat.

He looked over his shoulder at her, eyebrow cocked.

"Sorry... lo siento," she giggled nervously. "Cuando puedo... ver... las tortugas?" She'd taken a crash course in Spanish starting immediately after she found out she was coming here, and even with six months of intensive study, she was sure she'd mangled that.

The man looked back at her again and laughed. "I speak English. I was laughing at how eager you are."

"That's Rose in a nutshell," the other grad student on the trip, Peter, said from the front passenger seat. "She ruined the curve for our final exam."

"Should have studied harder," she shot back at him with a shrug. She turned her attention back to their driver. "What's your name, sir?"

"Arturo," he said. "I'm the facilities manager. We've got an hour drive to the research station – I'll show you your sleeping quarters and let you put down your bags, and then I can take you to the tortoise enclosure."

"I wouldn't mind a snack," Peter chimed in. He was second-ranked in the herpetology program, and if he were less concerned about his stomach, he might be first. But Rose wasn't here to compete with him – she was here to learn everything she could about the giant tortoises unique to this region, and help figure out how to save them from extinction. All in the three months between her first and second year of graduate school.

Her own stomach could wait.

The drive was fairly monotonous, more trees and cacti lining both sides of the road, but Rose found it fascinating nonetheless. Her heart was in her throat and she couldn't wait to see her first giant tortoise, up close and in person. She'd seen them from a distance in zoos, and of course in her textbooks... but she would actually be able to reach out and touch the ones living here.

Majestic creatures, and strange, more dinosaur than modern... They'd always captivated her, since she was a little girl and she used to test her luck with the snapping turtles that came out of the creek behind her house.

"You know what else I could use?" Peter said. "A shower. That was one hell of a plane trip."

Rose rolled her eyes in the direction of her window so he wouldn't see in the rear-view mirror. He cared about the science – she knew he did because she saw how carefully he worked – but he also had access to a rather generous trust fund and was entirely oblivious to the doors that it opened for him. Rose had spent the last semester working one job to pay for school, another to bank money for this trip, and juggling her coursework and Spanish lessons. Peter just packed his bags and assumed everything would work out.

True to Arturo's word, just under an hour later they were turning onto the dirt road that marked the entrance to the Charles Darwin Research Station. Rose stuck her head out her open window to take it all in. The facility had just opened earlier in the year, and so far, it was little more than a handful of pole buildings dropped into the jungle, with dirt paths between them. All around it, the Galapagos National Park was wild and green.

Arturo parked the Land Rover in front of a large building that was apparently the barracks, judging from the laundry line hanging outside of it.

"Here we are, home sweet home," he said, hopping out of the vehicle. "Barracks straight ahead – you can take any bed that's unoccupied." He turned to Rose. "There are a few other female scientists and staff members here, but not many. Your quarters are on the other side of the building – a bit cramped, unfortunately, but separated from the men."

"That's fine I won't be spending much time in bed," Rose said.

"The cafeteria is down that path," Arturo pointed to the left, and Peter put his hand on his stomach.

"Thank God."

"And the tortoises?" Rose asked.

Arturo laughed, looking at Peter. "You're right, she's a go-getter."

It was far from the worst thing she'd been called in her life, and Rose stood a little taller. Damn right she was – and she wasn't interested in losing another minute of her brief time here.

"Let's set down your bags, and I'll walk you over," Arturo promised.

Peter dropped his own luggage just inside the door of the men's side of the barracks, then practically sprinted for the cafeteria. Rose had a brief struggle with Arturo over who would carry her bags, and they settled for a compromise. She took her carry-on and he grabbed the duffel with most of her clothes.

"I appreciate the chivalry, but I'm sure I'll be doing much harder work than carrying my own things while I'm out here," she said. "I expect to be treated like every other scientist here."

"You may be wearing cargo pants and walking through the jungle, but you're still a lady," Arturo said, snatching the duffel from the back of the Land Rover.

Rose spared him another roll of the eyes. He meant well – most of the men in her life who treated her like she was too delicate to do the same work as them meant well. But if there was one thing she'd learned in her first year of graduate school, it was the importance of being seen as equal. No one would ever take her seriously as a scientist if they didn't even think her capable of carrying her own bags.

The two of them walked along the outside of the long building and came to a door on the other side. "There's the women's quarters," Arturo said, relinquishing her duffel bag. "I'll wait out here while you find a bunk."

"Thanks," Rose said. She left him in the sun and stepped into the welcome shade of the barracks.

There were about a dozen beds inside – actual bunk beds, she was surprised to find –with small wardrobes in between them. At this time of day there was no one else here, but the clothes and personal items left on various mattresses made it easy to tell which beds had been claimed. It looked like only about half of them were occupied, and Rose chose a lower bunk near a window, hoping for a nice nightly breeze.

She dumped her duffel on the floor beside the bed and set her carry-on on top of the mattress, then took a minute to dig through it to locate sunscreen. *Probably should have done this during the drive,* she thought as she slathered it on her bare arms and down her nose.

She heard the barracks door open and she called over her shoulder, "Just a moment, Arturo – I'm just lathering up."

"I'm not Arturo," a female voice answered.

Rose turned, excited to meet another female scientist. The woman standing before her was tall, with hair so short it approximated a man's cut. She was wearing a man's undershirt as well, and she was absolutely drenched in sweat. And Rose couldn't tear her eyes away.

"Hi, I'm Dee," the woman said, extending her hand.

Rose took it. Dee's eyes were a constellation of sparkling blue, and they captured her like no eyes ever had before. For a second, she couldn't remember what she was doing here, or even her own damn name.

Thankfully, it came back to her before the moment became awkward. "I'm Rose. I just got here."

Dee released her hand and nodded at the bunk she'd chosen. "I see that."

"Is that okay?" Rose asked, suddenly full of doubt. "Does that bed belong to someone?"

Dee chuckled. "It's all yours. I just meant because your stuff's so clean and tidy." She glanced down at the transparent sweat marks on her cotton shirt and shook her head. "You'll look like this by tomorrow. I just came in for a quick change before dinner. Hope I don't smell too bad."

"You smell fine," Rose said, her voice going weird and breathy. The only scents she'd picked up when Dee shook her hand were an earthiness and the sun-kissed smell of tanned skin. Dee had her back to her now, heading over to a bunk on the other side of the room. "What is it that you do here?"

"I'm an environmental scientist," she said. Dee explained more about her work, but Rose heard none of it because she was too distracted by the sight of Dee pulling a fresh cotton shirt out of her wardrobe and then peeling the sweat-drenched one off her back.

Rose quickly looked away.

"And you?"

"Hmm?"

When she looked back, Dee was clothed again and she had a wry, knowing look on her face. Like she'd been reading Rose's mind and knew what was swirling around in there. Impossible, because even Rose was confused about what she was feeling right now.

"What are you here to do?"

"Oh. I'm going to work with the giant tortoises," she said. Duh, weren't they what most everyone came here for? She added, "I'm a herpetologist... well, I will be. I'm in graduate school." Geez, run at the mouth much?

But Dee just smiled. "Cool. Well, I'm starving – I'll see you around."

"Yes," Rose agreed, watching Dee walk away, tall and full of all the confidence in the world. Meanwhile, Rose felt like she'd just been hit by a bus in the middle of the jungle. She wasn't the type to get flustered when meeting someone new, or to let anyone intimidate her. So why was she so immediately tongue-tied by Dee?

She was still standing there dumbly when Arturo popped his head in the door. "Knock-knock. You okay in here?"

"Sorry," she said, snapping out of it. "Coming."

"You have some gunk."

Rose frowned. "What?"

Arturo pointed to his nose and she caught her reflection in a mirror mounted on one of the wardrobes. Her nose was covered in sunscreen – she'd completely forgotten about it the moment Dee walked in and hadn't even attempted to blend it in.

Well, damn.

5
LAUREN

*B*y the following week, things had returned to normal at Sunnyside.

Gary went back to corporate and appeared to be happy with what he saw during his visit. Or at least Lauren had to assume that he was, because she hadn't gotten any emails or phone calls telling her to fix things. A small miracle given how many things were going wrong while Gary was here.

Lauren made a point of stopping in to Rose Moreno's room once a day to make sure she was settling in all right. Lauren did that with all the new residents, but she was particularly concerned about Rose. Between the emotional rollercoaster of a grim prognosis and her meddlesome daughter, Lauren worried about Rose's mental state.

"Has she been out of her room at all?" she asked Angelique one afternoon when things were slow.

Angelique shook her head. "Not for anything but

meals, but then, her daughter's been here almost every waking minute so I think they're just spending time together while they can."

Lauren nodded. "We'll have to make sure she meets the other residents at some point, makes some friends," Lauren said. "Maybe you can introduce her to Opal and Dee? They both like to make the rounds and visit with people."

"I'll see if I can get them seated together at dinner," Angelique said. "Although Dee and Opal are like oil and water, so maybe they'll have to meet separately."

"I'm sure you'll figure it out," Lauren said before heading off to her next task. "I appreciate you."

Working at Sunnyside was equal parts administration, conflict resolution, and matchmaking. Lauren was in charge of making sure it all ran smoothly, and half the time she felt more like a cruise director than someone working in the medical field.

That was why, on Friday night when she was clearing off her desk for the week, she paused when she came across the animal therapy pamphlets the woman with the fox had left behind. She'd actually forgotten all about the pamphlets, given how crazy that day had been, but she definitely hadn't forgotten the woman.

Grace, Lauren remembered her name. She had warm brown skin and bewitching grayish eyes. She was tall, with subtle curves, and she smelled like wildflowers. It was impossible to look away from her, even with a fox on her shoulder.

Striking. That was the word Lauren would use to describe her, if she could choose only one.

She settled back into her chair and picked up the pamphlets. They were packed with information, thoroughly cited from academic and medical journals. Grace had clearly done her homework, and by the time Lauren was done reading, she was convinced that Grace had a good argument for animal therapy for the elderly.

Gary had been clear on his position on the matter. *Get that thing out of here before it gives one of our residents Lyme disease.* But he'd barely even looked at Grace and her fox. He certainly hadn't read the pamphlets.

Besides, he was a numbers guy – he knew nothing about day-to-day life here at Sunnyside, or what would make the residents happy.

Lauren was here every single day. She saw the difference between a day when there was no programming scheduled and the residents wandered around listlessly, and a day when they had something to look forward to – like the string quartet last week. Hell, you could gauge the overall boredom levels from Opal's behavior alone. How many mini muffins got thrown? That was how long since the last scheduled entertainment.

Lauren glanced at her watch. It was a little after five, the end of the business day, but she picked up her desk phone anyway and called the number on Grace's business card.

"Hello?" Grace answered, then cleared her throat and added, "Williams Animal-Assisted Therapy, this is Grace speaking."

Lauren couldn't help smiling. "Hi, this is Lauren Carpenter from–"

"Sunnyside Senior Living," Grace said along with her. "I was hoping you'd call."

"You were?" The hopeful words came out before Lauren could bite them back. Now who was being unprofessional?

Grace cleared her throat. "Yes, I'd love to work with you. Did your boss change his mind?"

"Uh, not exactly," Lauren admitted. "But I'm interested."

"Oh?"

"In the program," Lauren clarified, although she *was* picturing Grace's smoky gray eyes as they talked.

How long had it been since her last date? She'd been so busy with the new job... it was probably when she'd first started here – and she'd inadvertently ghosted the poor woman for so long that she lost interest in Lauren.

"It seems like you did your research on Sunnyside," she went on, switching to business mode. "So you must know that mine is just one location owned by a larger corporation. I only have so much control over what programming we bring in, and given your business is therapeutic, that means there are even more restrictions."

"Yes, I have come across all that in my research," Grace confirmed. "If you're onboard, though, I'd love to team up to make the pitch to corporate along with you."

She was good – persistent and confident.

"Have you had luck with that in the past?" Lauren asked. She knew better than most how stubborn the people in corporate offices could be. Partly it was because they were so far removed from day-to-day life in the facilities. Mostly, though, it was because they all lived in fear of the L word – lawsuit.

For the first time, Grace hesitated on her end of the line. "Well, no. I haven't had the opportunity to try yet – full disclosure, Williams Animal-Assisted Therapy just launched last month–"

"Oh." Lauren felt herself deflate.

Grace kept going, though. "–but if you think this is something that can help your residents, I'll go to the ends of the earth and back to make sure they have access to it. I won't stop until–"

Lauren laughed. "Pause, pause. Before we start creating battle plans, maybe you better tell me more about how it works. It's more than just the fox, right?"

"Oh yeah, animal-assisted therapy is extremely customizable – I've got ideas for a variety of different programs I could bring in, and we can even set up your residents with individual companion animals if we can get corporate onboard." Grace was getting carried away on her own enthusiasm, and Lauren found herself nodding along with her – it was infectious. "You know what? This would be so much easier to explain in person. Could I take you out to dinner to talk more?"

Lauren stuttered. "Uhmm... dinner?"

"Or coffee? A beer?" Grace went on. "Spring water?"

Lauren laughed. "Dinner sounds nice. When are you free?"

"Tomorrow night?" Grace suggested. "There's a

noodle bar that just opened downtown that I've been dying to try."

"Pho Real?" Lauren asked. "Yeah, I've been there – it's excellent. I can meet you at six if that works?"

"It's a date," Grace said. Then her self-consciousness came adorably back to the surface. "A work date, I mean. I'll bring my presentation."

They hung up, and Lauren stacked Grace's pamphlets and business card neatly on the corner of her desk. What the hell was she doing? She could tell herself it was about the animals and her residents all she wanted, but the fact remained that Gary had said no. And Gary never changed his mind once he was convinced something was a liability.

"Am I wasting that poor woman's time?" Lauren wondered aloud as she packed her bag to go home. And a little voice in the back of her head asked, *Are you wasting your own?*

There had been a definite spark between them – Lauren was sure it was mutual when they met in person, and she could even feel it over the phone. But she had no time or energy to date. Setting up this meeting with Grace – whether it really was just a work meeting or not – was pointless. There could be nothing more.

Not in this lifetime, anyway.

And, as if to remind her just how busy she was, her phone rang. The display said *Nurses' Station 3*. Lauren sighed, set down her bag, and picked up the phone.

"Oh, thank God you're still here," the night shift

nurse said. "You're never gonna guess what Opal just did…"

The following evening, Lauren stood on the sidewalk outside Pho Real, adjusting her skirt and wondering if she should have made this a lunch meeting. Dinner was so formal, so date-ish.

I hope she actually brings a presentation, she thought as she tugged on the neckline of her top. She was wearing a sleek crimson pencil skirt and a floral blouse that she'd originally bought for work, but immediately realized was too revealing. The neckline plunged too far to be professional, and there were a handful of male residents at Sunnyside who weren't shy about pointing that out. The 'horny old man' stereotype existed for a reason, and Lauren preferred not to give them any ammunition.

Still, it was a pretty blouse with a wrap-around tie that flattered her curves, and it was a shame to relegate it to the back of her closet. She'd debated for far too long while she was picking her outfit for this meeting, then got frustrated at how fussy she was being and just put the blouse on.

Now, she was thinking it was too much again.

"Lauren?"

She turned at her name, glad that Grace was here and whether or not she was appropriately dressed was now out of her hands. It was what it was.

"Oh wow, you look stunning," Grace said, her eyes

sweeping briefly over her. That gaze felt nothing like being looked over by an octogenarian – in fact, Lauren would have been happy to bask in it even longer. But Grace politely held her hand out. "It's nice to see you again, Lauren."

Name sounding velvety on her tongue.

"You too, Grace," she said, taking an indulgent moment to drink the other woman in since Grace had looked her over first.

She was wearing all black, trousers that accentuated her long legs and a light suit jacket with a simple V-neck beneath it that showed off a tantalizing amount of skin at her own chest. The touches of feminine contrasted perfectly with the overall masculine cut of her outfit.

"No Sonic tonight?" Lauren asked.

"Figured the restaurant wouldn't appreciate him," Grace said. "It's shedding season." She opened the door for Lauren, then added, "Besides, he's not mine – he belongs to a friend. I just borrow him whenever I need an irresistibly cute animal."

Lauren gave her a wry smile over her shoulder. "Feeling confident tonight, then?"

Grace smirked back at her. "You already said yes to the date. I figured now I'll dazzle you with data. And if that doesn't work, I've got a hamster in my breast pocket."

Lauren laughed. "You don't really, do you?"

"Two?" the hostess interrupted.

"Yes," Grace answered, ignoring Lauren's question but throwing her a wink.

The hostess led them through the small restaurant to

a booth along one wall, and left them with menus. As soon as Lauren was seated across from Grace, she leaned in and whispered, "Seriously, do you have a hamster in your pocket?"

"I guess you'll just have to wait and find out," Grace shot back with a self-satisfied grin.

"You're a tease," Lauren said, losing all semblance of professionalism. When was the last time she'd been with someone that she fell into such an easy camaraderie with? Ages.

They ordered – beef pho for Lauren and a ramen bowl for Grace – and then Grace dug into her ever-present satchel and produced a tablet.

"Shall we get the business out of the way before the food gets here?" she suggested. "I brought visual aids, as promised."

"Sure, give me your best pitch," Lauren said. She leaned forward, and Grace turned her tablet sideways, tapping somewhat awkwardly while she cued up her presentation. Then she frowned.

"Do you mind if I sit beside you? It'd be so much easier for us both to see."

Lauren scooted toward the wall and patted the bench seat beside her. "Come on over."

Grace slid in beside her, the scent of wildflowers drifting into Lauren's nose. *Be professional,* she reminded herself. They'd been having fun flirting with each other, but the purpose of this dinner was for Grace to pitch her business. If Lauren was going into it knowing the chances of convincing Gary were slim to none, the least she could do was be a good audience.

"Ready?" Grace asked, those smoky eyes glimmering with enthusiasm.

"Whenever you are."

Grace spent the next fifteen minutes breathlessly explaining her business, and the animal-assisted therapy concept in general. Her passion for the subject was evident, and Lauren was really enjoying listening to her talk. When their food came, she was sad to see Grace go back to her side of the booth.

"Was that too much information?" she asked as she put away the tablet and picked up a pair of chopsticks.

Lauren smiled. "Don't ask me to recite any of the facts, but I thought it was a really good pitch. I'm sold on animal-assisted therapy being beneficial for elderly populations. How did you get into this type of work, anyway?"

Grace's eyes clouded for the first time all night.

"Is it a touchy subject?" Lauren frowned, surprised.

"No," Grace said, though her facial expression told Lauren a different story. "My dad passed a year ago and he was a big animal-lover. He's the reason I went into veterinary medicine."

"I'm sorry for your loss," Lauren said, feeling the inadequacy of the words.

"Thank you." Grace took a breath, then her bright smile was back. "Anyway, I'd much rather talk to you about how I can help your residents... or maybe we can switch to more casual subjects, like what you do when you're not working?"

Lauren smiled, but she didn't have a good answer for that. "Ever since I got this job, I don't really have time when I'm not working. I'm either at Sunnyside or I'm on call."

"That can't be healthy."

"It probably isn't," Lauren said, even though she knew damn well it wasn't. "But if we keep talking about personal things, I won't be able to write off this dinner as a work expense."

"I'd much rather it be a date," Grace said, her foot nudging Lauren's beneath the table. "Let me pick up the check, and in the meantime you can tell me what you *would* do if you *did* have free time."

Lauren smiled. "This."

6
GRACE

Grace walked away from dinner with Lauren not quite knowing how to feel.

On one hand, she was sure that she'd won Lauren over to her program, and she'd promised to arrange a little field trip for the two of them so that Lauren could see her in action. Grace was co-hosting a bunny yoga session along with a friend of hers who ran a rabbit rescue, and Lauren was going to come see how Grace operated. She was one step closer to cementing a partnership with Sunnyside, or at least the Granville location, which would really launch her business into successful territory.

But on the other hand... the minute she saw Lauren's name pop up on her phone yesterday, her belly had grown warm with desire. The woman was seriously gorgeous, and seeing her in that tight skirt and plunging neckline... *damn*.

Grace was sure that the feeling was mutual. She'd

noticed Lauren checking her out as she sauntered up the sidewalk outside the restaurant, and she could practically feel Lauren's heart racing when they sat beside each other in the booth. Every time Grace tried to steer the conversation into personal topics, though, Lauren had pumped the brakes.

They'd parted ways very professionally after dinner, with a firm handshake and a promise to meet up at Wakefield Rabbit Rescue later in the week. And Grace had spent the last couple of days trying her damnedest not to want more than what she'd gotten.

It was greedy, right?

Lauren was already going out of her way to give Grace's business a chance, even after her boss nixed it.

And yet all Grace could think about was how soft Lauren's dark curls would feel between her fingers, and how much she wanted to hook one hand behind Lauren's neck and pull her into a kiss. She was at least six inches shorter than Grace and it would feel so nice to wrap Lauren up in her arms...

Stop, she told herself for the hundredth time.

Now, she was pulling up the long gravel driveway of the farm the rescue operated out of. It was in a little town called Camden, about thirty minutes outside the city, and this was only the third bunny yoga session that Grace had led. She needed to stop thinking about Lauren's cute little lips and focus on her job.

She parked beside the big barn that housed all the rescue rabbits, and before she was even out of her car, her friend the rescue owner was bounding down the steps of the farmhouse.

"Parker, hey," Grace said. "How are you?"

"Great," she said. "Adopted out one of our special needs bunnies last night and I just got a video from his new owner – he's settling in well already."

She held up her phone and Grace saw a three-legged tawny-colored rabbit tentatively hopping around an area scattered with chew toys. "Aww, he looks curious."

"He came to me neglected and with a bad infection," Parker said. "Amputation was really the only choice at that point, but he adapted so quickly. It hasn't slowed him down at all."

"That's sweet," Grace said. "Also, fuck whoever neglected him in the first place."

"Indeed," Parker agreed. "Anyway, I have a whole barn full of eligible adoptees who can't wait to do yoga today. Want to help me get them moved over to the outdoor run?"

"Yep, I remember the drill."

Together, they carried about a dozen rabbits from the barn to a large fenced area in the yard. Parker went into the farmhouse to get her pet rabbit, a foster fail named Lucky, so he could join in the fun, and Grace leaned against the fence to watch them all run and play while she waited for her yogis to arrive.

"Same group as last time?" Parker asked after depositing Lucky among his outdoor friends.

"Yeah, the anxiety and depression patients," Grace said. "I heard from a few of them after our last session –

they said the bunnies really helped relax them, and not just during the session but after too."

"That's great," Parker said. "Well, my babies are available whenever you need them. Especially if they end up bonding and getting adopted in the process."

"I appreciate it," Grace said. She heard gravel crunching and turned toward the driveway. She recognized Lauren's car from the Sunnyside lot – it was a memorable burnt orange. "Oh, one more thing."

"Yeah?"

"I invited a friend."

"A lady friend?"

Grace winced. She *had* said that with a weird, awkward inflection. "Not exactly. She's the director of an assisted living facility I'm trying to get some animals into. I wanted her to see what I do."

Parker winked at her. "Right, I gotcha. I'll make sure you look good." Grace was about to object, but the car pulled up next to hers and the engine cut out. Parker asked, "What's her name?"

"Lauren," Grace said, and as if summoned, the dark-haired beauty emerged from the car.

"Hi, I hope you don't mind me coming early," she called. "I thought you might talk me through what you're doing."

"She's cute," Parker said under her breath, then they both went to greet the new arrival.

Lauren was dressed in a tight pair of leggings with a geometric pattern on them that drew Grace's eye – it was definitely the design and not their curve-hugging properties. For sure. Lauren had a yoga mat rolled up and tucked under her arm as well, and Grace said, "Let me guess – not a yoga novice?"

"I've done a down-dog or two in my day," Lauren said, then she seemed to notice that it wasn't just the two of them standing out here. She extended her hand to Parker. "I'm Lauren Carpenter. Thanks for having me."

"Parker Rose-Wakefield, crazy bunny lady," she answered. "Happy to have you."

The three of them walked over to the run, and Grace explained that today's session wasn't likely to make Lauren break a sweat. "We've got a certified yoga instructor who'll be here shortly to lead the class, but it's a pretty laid-back session. It's geared to people struggling with anxiety and depression, so it's less aerobic and more about just stretching and practicing mindfulness."

"The bunnies help with that," Parker added. "It's really hard to get lost in your thoughts when you're doing a plank and all of a sudden there's a rabbit on your back."

"Better than a monkey, I bet," Lauren said.

Another car pulled into the driveway, and Grace recognized it as the instructor's. She excused herself to go meet her at the barn, leaving Lauren and Parker to make small talk for a moment.

A few clients started arriving as well, and Grace got swept up in running the session. She made sure Lauren found a spot and felt free to participate, but mostly she had to focus on her clients for the next hour. The instructor took a spot at the front of the outdoor space, and Parker and Grace both circulated throughout the session to make sure the rabbits visited everyone and didn't chew any yoga mats.

The next time Grace got a chance to talk to Lauren, bunny yoga was over and most of the clients as well as the instructor had departed.

"I'm so sorry I got swamped, I didn't really explain like you wanted me to," Grace apologized as she met Lauren at her mat. She was rolling it up, and a curious lop was sniffing at her leggings. "What did you think?"

"I loved it," Lauren said. "I'll be honest, I wasn't sure how having to worry about accidentally kicking a rabbit while doing a sun salutation was going to be relaxing, but it actually was!"

Grace chuckled. "Yeah, I heard that a lot after the first couple of sessions. But bunnies are really good at getting out of the way – they're prey animals, it's instinctual." She scooped up the lop and handed it to Lauren, then took her yoga mat for her. "Do you want to stick around a little longer, help us get the bunnies back in the barn? You can pick my brain some more about the program if you want – and Parker's too, she's been instrumental in getting this running smoothly."

"I'd love to," Lauren said, nuzzling the extra-soft fur at the little white bunny's neck and making Grace irrationally jealous. "I got to talk to a couple of the clients too, before they left. They gave glowing reviews."

"Good," Grace said. "So, do you think something like this could help your residents at Sunnyside, if you had approval from corporate?"

"Absolutely," Lauren said, "but Gary's a bit of a stick

in the mud. I don't really know what I can do to convince him."

"Would a bunny help?" Grace asked.

Lauren laughed. "If it were anyone else, I'm sure it would. I'm not sure Gary's even human, though – he's more like a cyborg that feeds on spreadsheets and corporate policies."

"Well, let me put your yoga mat in your car and I'll come back to wrangle some bunnies," Grace offered. Lauren handed Grace her keys so she could get into the trunk, then waited inside the fence with the lop in her arms.

When Grace got back, she found Lauren talking to Parker about Sunnyside.

"I would love to bring the bunnies sometime," Parker said. "Events like these are a win-win-win for me. More people learn about the rescue, the bunnies get socialized, and sometimes they bond so well they end up getting adopted."

"I'm not sure there can be any adoptions when it comes to Sunnyside," Lauren said. "Although I'm getting pretty attached to this little guy."

Parker grinned. "My plan for world bunny domination is working. Come on, you can give him a treat in the barn."

Grace scooped up the nearest rabbit – a black and white Dutch that squirmed in her arms – and followed them to the barn. Inside, there were roomy pens for all the rabbits. The ones who got along were housed together, and the less social ones had pens all to themselves. Grace set down the Dutch rabbit where Parker told her to, then watched Lauren kiss the lop on the head and give him one of the homemade treats Parker handed her.

"Okay, I'm in love," Lauren said, reluctantly setting the rabbit down.

Me too, Grace thought, then quickly pushed the idea aside. It was obviously hyperbole – they'd only known each other a few days, and developing feelings for Lauren was ill-advised because she was trying to work with her professionally. But that didn't stop her heart from swelling when she watched her so tenderly cuddling a little cotton ball of a rabbit... and other parts of her warmed up when her eyes fell to those skin-tight leggings.

"You should adopt him," Parker said. "Seems like he likes you too."

Lauren shook her head. "I'm never at home – it wouldn't be fair to him."

"Could be good motivation to work a little less," Grace teased with a wink.

"Come on," Parker said. "We've got about eight more bunnies to go."

She headed back outside and Grace let her shoulder brush up against Lauren's as they followed. "Having fun?"

"Yeah, this is wonderful," Lauren said. "I can't remember the last time I slowed down and took a breath like this."

"I'd be happy to remind you more often," Grace said. "You don't want to get burned out."

Lauren laughed. "I can't afford to."

"I don't think that's how it works," Grace pointed out, and this time, Lauren was the one who brushed against Grace, just before they emerged into the sunshine and turned their attention back to bunny-herding.

7

LAUREN

Lauren knew that if she was going to make sure Grace didn't waste her time – and keep her own residents' best interests at heart – she really should call corporate and try to talk Gary into the idea of bringing animals into Sunnyside. But every time she thought about calling him and trying to convince him no one was going to end up with Lyme disease, she knew it would be like talking to a brick wall.

She talked it over with Angelique and a few of the other nurses first, getting their medical opinion since Lauren was an administrator, not a doctor. And she talked to a handful of residents she knew would give their honest opinion without getting their hopes up in case it didn't work out. They were all excited about the idea, and seeing the light come into the residents' eyes at the mere mention of animals was enough to tell Lauren this was something Sunnyside needed.

"I had Springer Spaniels for most of my adult life,"

Dee, one of the residents Lauren confided in, said, a sappy smile taking over her face. "Such smart dogs, and they love to cuddle. My last one passed about five years before I came here and I still miss her."

"I always had cats," another resident, Anita, said. "My daughter took in my Dottie, but she hasn't bonded with the family the way she did with me. I wish I could go visit her more often."

Or bring her here for little visits, Lauren thought. Some assisted living facilities allowed pets – Sunnyside had never been one of those, though, and she got the impression it was purely because it was easier to say no than to work through the issues that would arise from saying yes.

"So, do you think it would make you happier to be able to visit with animals now and then?" Lauren asked. She barely finished the question before the emphatic responses came.

"I got to pet that fox that was here last week," one of the nurses said. "I wish he could have stayed longer!"

"A fox?" Anita asked, perking up.

"You would not believe how soft he was!" the nurse said, and the conversation veered into a recap of everything Grace had told her about fennecs in the short time that she'd been waiting in the hall for Lauren.

So, the opinions were unanimous, from both the staff and the residents – animals would brighten up Sunnyside and the research regarding the benefits was overwhelmingly positive. All Lauren had to do was step in front of the corporate firing squad and convince Gary it was a good idea.

She waited until noon on the day she'd resolved to make the call. Gary was a very punctual man and he took his lunch breaks like clockwork. Lauren was hoping to get his answering machine – she could make her initial pitch there, then field objections when he returned her call.

The phone rang twice, then Gary's gruff voice was in her ear. "Peterson."

Lauren stumbled for a second, caught off guard. Damn it, the one time he wasn't out the door at twelve o'clock sharp?

"Hello?"

"Hi, Mr. Peterson, this is Lauren Carpenter from the Granville–"

"I know, I see your caller ID," he said. "I'm on the road, coming back from our Toledo location. What's up?"

Ah, so that explained it. Lauren could just picture him sitting ramrod-straight at the wheel, hands at ten and two just like they taught in driving school. "I can call back if you're busy."

"Far from it, the drive is monotonous. Is there a problem?"

"No," she said. *Aside from the fact that this call is going the opposite of how I envisioned it.* "I wanted to talk to you about a program that would be very beneficial for my residents – it's a form of therapy that's been gaining popularity and I've had the opportunity to see it in action."

She'd decided that Gary's busy schedule could work

to her benefit – she was going to pitch Grace's business as if he'd never laid eyes on a fennec fox at Sunnyside, as if he hadn't already vetoed it. Maybe he'd have forgotten by now.

"I'm listening."

"There's a growing body of research regarding the effectiveness of animal-assisted ther–"

"No."

Damn it!

"Mr. Peterson–"

"Is this about that fox?" he asked. "I already told you there's far too much liability involved."

"They're not Lyme carriers," Lauren argued. "And it doesn't have to be a fox. This weekend I went to bunny yoga–"

"It's not going to happen, Lauren," he said. Yep, brick wall. Lauren had just crashed into it at sixty miles an hour, and it didn't feel good.

"Sir–"

"No," he said again. "We can discuss it further at my next quarterly visit if you really want to, but the answer will be the same. I'm sorry."

Like hell you are, Lauren thought. She was far too pragmatic to say that out loud, though. Instead, she forced herself to smile so that she wouldn't sound as frustrated as she felt. "Okay, thank you for your time."

"No problem," he said, sounding as if he actually felt he'd done her a favor. "Is there anything else?"

"No."

"All right," he said. "I'll see you in two and a half months. Call if you need anything in the meantime."

"Sure. Drive safe."

Lauren heard the click of the call disconnecting, and set down the receiver. Son of a bitch. That had gone about as well as she'd expected it to, and yet deep down she'd actually been hopeful that she'd be able to win him over.

Hell, she hadn't even gotten to make any of the arguments she'd prepared. She had Grace's pamphlets and statistics, and the input of the staff and residents. She had numbers, and Gary loved numbers. But all she'd gotten was no, no, no.

"Fuck you, Gary," she grumbled under her breath.

She sat there frustrated and stewing for about five minutes. For the first nine months she'd worked here, she'd been a model employee, doing every little thing that Gary asked of her and making him look good for all the other corporate overlords. And the first time she had an idea to improve the lives of her residents, he stonewalled her.

Lauren made a decision – one that scared the hell out of her. With her pulse speeding up, she picked up her phone again.

Gary was a bureaucrat. He had his nose in spreadsheets ninety percent of the time, and more importantly, he wasn't coming back to Granville for nearly three months. Lauren was the one who knew what her residents needed... if she could *prove* to him at his next visit that animal-assisted therapy was having a positive impact, maybe he'd actually listen to her. Maybe she could make him see what she already knew – this was worth the risk.

Her hand was actually shaking a little bit as she started to dial. Lauren was a rule-follower. She toed the line and did what people told her to do. The phrase 'it's better to beg forgiveness than ask permission' gave her heart palpitations.

But she *knew* this was right.

"Williams Animal-Assisted Therapy," Grace answered.

"Hey, it's me," Lauren said, heart fluttering in her chest. "I want to schedule a session for my residents."

8
DEE

*E*very time Dee walked by Rose's room over the next week, either her door was closed or her daughter was there and she gave Dee such a death stare that it was clear she best move along before she spontaneously combust.

It was nice that Rose's daughter visited often – there were dozens of people here whose relatives seemed to be under the impression that Sunnyside's doors only opened in one direction, and they never came to visit. And then there were people like Dee, who didn't have anyone left to come see her.

But now there was Rose.

What was she doing here?

After the first time Dee locked eyes with her, she'd racked her brain to remember where Rose lived back when they knew each other. They'd both been working on Santa Cruz Island in the Galapagos back then, and they had so little time together – Rose was a grad student only there for the summer. The intensity and urgency of their affair had left little time for details about their normal lives.

And afterward...

Dee's heart constricted in her chest thinking about it, even after all these years. Fifty-eight of them, to be exact.

That was why she'd spent so much time lingering in the hallway outside of Rose's apartment, trying to get another look at her. Trying to talk to her. She'd even resorted to googling Rose with both her maiden name and her new last name, but there was precious little information about her online.

That wasn't overly surprising. Dee was pleased to see that Rose Dennison had published a number of academic papers over a lengthy career as a professor of herpetology. Like a lot of scientists, she must have continued publishing under her maiden name even after she got married. Rose Moreno, on the other hand, didn't have much of an internet presence. Were they one and the same?

In her heart, Dee knew that they were. She'd felt the same connection she had all those years ago the moment their eyes met. It was like stepping into a time machine and being transported across decades and thousands of miles in a second, to the barracks where they first met.

But logically... what was she doing here? What were the odds?

Was this it? Was Dee finally losing her marbles?

It didn't help that Gina kept Rose in her suite nearly all the time, and even brought her meals there.

One afternoon when things were quiet and Cora was too sleepy to continue her romance novel, Dee made her way to the nurses' station and leaned casually on the counter. "How are you today, Angelique?" she asked with her most winning smile.

Angelique rolled her eyes. "I know that tone – what are you buttering me up for?"

Dee put a hand to her chest. "Am I not allowed to ask you how you're doing?"

"Not like that," Angelique said, gesturing to Dee's overall posture. "What's up?"

"Well, I'm curious about our newest addition," Dee said. "She's not very social, is she?"

Angelique frowned. "No, I've been keeping an eye on her – I was hoping she'd venture out for meals more, but I don't think she's feeling very good."

Dee's chest felt heavy. "Is she sick?"

The thought hadn't occurred to her. Rose *had* looked small and frail in her recliner, but Opal was probably eighty pounds soaking wet and that didn't stop her from being a right terror who would likely wind up breaking Guinness records with her age.

"You know I can't tell you that, Dee," Angelique said. "Privacy rules."

Dee grunted. "Right." She tapped on the counter, thinking.

"Lauren's been trying to get Rose to be more active," Angelique offered. "If you want to meet her, I'll let you know if she decides to come to any of the scheduled activities."

"Okay, thanks," Dee said. "Anyway, how are you? I really did want to know."

Angelique smiled. "You're one of the good ones, Dee."

Dee had to wait two more weeks before she finally got her chance to talk to Rose. She'd nearly given up, thinking Rose's protective daughter was never going to let her out of her sight – or out of her room.

Could fate really be that cruel, separating the two of them for *almost* a lifetime, then giving Dee one last glimpse of the woman who'd stolen her heart all those years ago... only to keep them separated by the width of a flimsy door? Dee told herself again and again that she was mistaken – losing her mind, even. This Rose was not *her* Rose.

But at her core, she knew.

Knew from the moment their eyes met.

It was *her*.

And finally, the window of opportunity to confirm it opened.

It was a rainy Thursday, the type of day that made people shiftless because it reminded them how long the hours could drag on for. Dee had spent her morning reading to Cora, until she noticed her friend had nodded off, and then Dee set the tablet in her lap and did the same. The rain always that effect on her, even when she was young.

The afternoon held promise, though. There was a new activity coming, something that Sunnyside had never had before – puppy playtime. Flyers had popped up all over the building over the last few days advertising the event, and a lot of the residents had been eagerly talking about it.

Dee was looking forward to it. When was the last time a dog had bounded into her lap, its limitless energy exploding all over the place? She missed her Springer Spaniels, but after the last one passed, she knew she was too old to get another. Puppy playtime, though… she could practically smell the puppy breath already.

When it was time, she woke Cora and pushed her in her wheelchair to the largest of the common rooms, where a lot of residents were already gathered.

"Do you think they'll notice if I smuggle a dog back to my room?" Opal was asking.

"They probably know how many they've got," the old man next to her answered.

"Well, I brought my biggest knitting bag just in case," Opal said with a wink. "Though I do wish it was kitty playtime."

Dee was just locking Cora's wheels in place on the periphery of the room when Lauren came in holding an animal carrier, followed by a whole train of people with more carriers. Residents started cooing and crowding around as they caught glimpses of the puppies within, and the whole room erupted with cuteness overload.

"Everybody take a couple steps back, please," Lauren called loudly. "We're going to bring the dogs in then close the doors, can't have them running loose through the halls. But they'll have toys and treats and free roam of the room to come visit you."

Hardly anybody actually gave her space to get situated. The excitement was palpable, and if Dee hadn't felt the duty to stick next to the stationary Cora, she probably would have been crowding right in there with them. She could hear tiny, spirited barks coming from the carriers, and she strained her neck to get a peek.

"Go ahead, dear," Cora said. "Enjoy yourself."

"They're not even finished bringing them in," Dee said. "I'll stay here with you."

"I'm not being altruistic," Cora pointed out. "I need you to be my legs – get in there and nab me a puppy."

Dee laughed. "I'll do my best."

There were about a dozen carriers when all was said and done, and four human volunteers. Lauren introduced them all, including the tall, dark-skinned, pretty woman who'd been here before with a fox perched on her shoulder. Her name was like a description of her – Grace – and in her much younger days, Dee might well have approached her in a bar. She exuded confidence and kindness, much like Lauren, and who could resist a gorgeous woman holding a cute animal?

"All these puppies are future service animals," Grace explained, snuggling up to a golden retriever she'd lifted from its carrier. "They've just begun their training, and the first step is to get them comfortable with people. You're doing them a favor by playing with them today –

you're helping them become the best workers they can be for their future humans."

The other two volunteers brought in the promised toys and treats then headed out, closing the double doors behind them.

"Feel free to play, everyone," Lauren said. "If you need someone to bring you a puppy, just flag me or Grace down."

"Ah, this is the life," Opal said, raising her hand and snapping her fingers in the air. "Bring me a puppy!"

Grace laughed and deposited her golden in Opal's lap. It immediately put its paws on her chest and started licking her face, and Opal was clearly in puppy heaven. Lauren and Grace opened the rest of the carriers and that puppy energy Dee had been craving burst into the room. There were several different breeds, and some of the carriers held more than one dog. Some of the more agile residents got down on the floor with them, and Dee went to select one for her and Cora to play with.

She didn't see any Springer Spaniels, but she did spot a German Shepherd with adorably perky ears. She scooped him into her arms, then turned to go back to Cora.

And paused mid-step.

Even in the chaos of the room, her eyes went immediately to Rose sitting in the back, her daughter beside her. When had they come in? Rose wasn't there when Dee arrived – she was sure of that. Rose met Dee's gaze, as if the same magnetic pull had drawn her own attention, but then she looked away.

"Dee?" Cora called. "You okay?"

Heart sinking, Dee brought the German Shepherd to her friend. Rose didn't even want to look at her. Had she forgotten their summer together?

Dee set the puppy in Cora's lap, then sat heavily beside her. Cora let herself be distracted by the big bundle of fluff in her arms for a few moments, then nudged Dee. "What's wrong?"

"Nothing," Dee lied.

"Go get yourself a puppy, then," Cora said. "You've been looking forward to this for days."

She shuffled slowly back to the center of the room, and this time a curly-haired pup came to her, something in the poodle family. She grabbed a handful of kibble, then chose a seat nearby, dropping a trail of dog food so the puppy would follow her. Thanks to her hip, getting down on the ground was no longer an option, but this was the first time she'd seen Rose out of her room. Dee wanted a chair facing her, so she could peek her way now and again.

Convince herself that this was not *her* Rose, if at all possible.

She held out a piece of kibble and the puppy tried to snatch at it.

"Sit," Dee said, testing its training. The puppy just wagged its tail and made another lunge for the kibble, so Dee decided it'd probably had none. "Sit," she repeated, pushing down on its hind quarters.

Rose had a pure white fluffy thing in her lap – a Great Pyrenees, maybe? Dee wasn't looking at the dog, though.

Rose's whole face was lit up with happiness, and that smile… it was etched into Dee's heart. It'd been almost six decades, and yet it was indelible. There was not a shred of doubt left that, as unlikely as it was, as impossible to explain as it was, the woman Dee had fallen in love with fifty-eight years ago on another continent, for one brief and beautiful summer, was sitting across the room with a puppy in her lap.

And a relentless gatekeeper sitting to her right.

Dee couldn't stop stealing glances, but Rose never looked back in her direction. The same could not be said for her daughter, who shot narrowed glances at Dee on more than one occasion.

"What's her problem?" Dee asked the poodle at her feet. "I've never even met her. Sit." The puppy did, and she rewarded him with a couple pieces of kibble. "Good boy!"

He was a fast learner, and she had no doubt he'd be a star pupil in guide dog school. Even with her attention divided between the puppy, Rose and Rose's daughter, Dee had him sitting on command by the end of the hour, and she'd stood up and started to teach him to heel as well.

Though, she might have had an ulterior motive for that one. It allowed her to move about the room, and get closer to Rose. That was how she happened to overhear Rose's daughter when she took a phone call.

She got up and walked to the corner of the room, one hand pressed to her ear to drown out all the barking, lifting the cell phone to her other ear. Dee had better manners than to eavesdrop, but she just happened to be walking the puppy in that direction anyway... how could she help it?

"This is Gina," Rose's daughter huffed as she answered the call. "... Why can't you handle that? ... But isn't it Todd's job to–" A sigh, loud enough to make her annoyance known to the person on the other end of the line. "Okay, fine, I'm on my way."

She ended the call and looked up before Dee could make her escape. They locked eyes, and Dee offered a sympathetic smile. "Work problems?"

Gina narrowed her eyes. "Do you always listen in on strangers' conversations?"

Okay, that was probably deserved. "Sorry," Dee said, and did an about-face, calling her puppy to heel. They made their way back across the room and Dee decided to work on 'sit' some more. She reclaimed her chair, keeping her head bowed as she peeked through her lashes at Rose and her daughter.

Gina was trying to take Rose back to her room. If she couldn't stay, apparently neither could Rose. She put her hands on the Great Pyrenees, and anguish broke across Rose's face. It made Dee's chest tighten, and she was damn near ready to go over there and give Gina a piece of her mind – stranger or not. But then Lauren came to the rescue.

"Everything okay?" she asked, her voice louder than it needed to be so Dee ended up hearing every word. That was what happened when half the people you talked to in a given day were hearing impaired – and it worked to Dee's favor now.

She couldn't hear what Rose or Gina said, but she got the gist from Lauren's end of the conversation.

"The dogs are only here for another ten minutes," she said. "You might as well stay, Rose... I can make sure you get back to your room afterward... It's no trouble."

Dee read Rose and Gina's expressions to fill in their words. Rose was relieved, petting and cuddling her new furry friend. Gina was annoyed at being overridden – probably used to getting her way – but this was not the hill she was going to die on. Anyway, she had to get to work to do Todd's job, so she gave in, kissed the top of her mother's head, and left.

Dee wasted no time seizing the one and only opportunity she was likely to get.

"Okay, buddy, this was fun and I hope to see you again, but I gotta go," she said to the poodle, laying the rest of the kibble in a mound on a nearby chair. The puppy dove right into it and barely noticed her leaving.

Dee shuffled as fast as her bad hip would allow over to Rose's side of the room.

"Hi," she said. "Lauren, I can help her get back to her room after if you have other things to do."

Like an entire room full of puppies to corral.

Dee was past pretending she hadn't been eavesdropping, and Lauren looked relieved at the offer. "That would be great, thank you. Rose, have you met Dee?"

Their eyes locked, and once again Dee felt herself

being swept across time and space, back to the Galapagos. To the best summer of her life.

Rose held out her hand. Dee took it, shock rippling through her at how paper-thin her skin was, how frail she looked. *Oh yeah, we're old now,* she thought. And Rose said, "It's nice to meet you, Dee."

Lauren walked away, satisfied with her introductions, but confusion speared through Dee. She studied Rose's gaze — there was recognition there, she was sure of it. And the door-slamming daughter was nowhere around, so why pretend she didn't know her?

Rose released her hand and Dee sat down beside her. "You remember me, right?"

God, it was going to break her heart if she had to spell it all out. *You know, from the three months of romance and mind-blowing sex every time we got a chance to sneak away together? I know it was a long time ago, and maybe I'm being egotistical, but I didn't think it was possible to forget. I sure haven't.*

Rose shook her head. "I just moved in here. We've never met before."

Did she have dementia? Or was Dee so insignificant in her life that she truly had forgotten her?

"We have," Dee said. "On Santa Cruz Island."

Rose shook her head again and turned her attention back to the white puff ball still in her lap. "I'm sorry, but you're mistaken."

9
ROSE
1964

It took Rose all of a week to find herself alone with Dee, and only a few minutes more to let Dee take her hand and pull her in for a kiss.

It was the first time she'd ever kissed a woman. For that matter, she'd only had a few chaste kisses with the boys she'd gone out with in high school and college too. She was always far too busy for trivial things like dating, and none of those boys had set her world on fire anyway.

Dee, though... she was different.

Rose found her eyes drawn to her every single time they were in a room together, whether they were wolfing down meals in the cafeteria or lying in their bunks in the barracks or passing each other on the trails that wove through the research station. Dee's work rarely took her to the tortoise enclosure where Rose spent most of her days. But when their paths did cross... she took Rose's breath away merely by her presence.

How could anyone have that much power?

At first Rose put it down to exhaustion and dehydration. She *had* just finished a pretty tiresome journey of many hours, and she'd encountered Dee in the first moment of down-time she'd had all day. She was practically delirious and could not be held accountable for her thoughts.

But the next time Rose met Dee, it was after a hearty meal and a cool shower and a change of clothes. The whole barracks was getting ready for bed and Rose had met all the other female scientists and staff members too, but Dee was the one her head kept turning back to.

Was it admiration? An innocent crush on a woman who was a little further down the career path Rose had been yearning for her whole life?

If it was, why did she spend so much time looking at the supple curves of Dee's lips when she spoke? Why did she like the earthy, rich smell of her so much?

Rose tried to ignore her for a few days after that. Not because of the way she was feeling for another woman – although her conservative parents back in Indiana certainly wouldn't be happy to learn about that aspect of her summer internship. No, she mostly ignored Dee because she couldn't afford to be distracted. She had twelve short weeks out here to soak up as much knowledge and experience as she could, and she'd be damned if *anything* threw her off her path.

And it was working, for a few days at least.

Rose learned that Dee woke up early most days, and was out of the barracks before most of the other women's alarms even went off. She was studying the temperature changes on the island, and it was important to get readings early in the day – which was convenient for Rose. That left only lunchtime in the cafeteria and bedtime in the barracks to reckon with.

She grabbed extra food during breakfast, squirreling it away in her backpack and eating lunch with the tortoises, Frank and Margaret. That turned out to be a boon, anyway – she started sharing her salads and fruit with them, and they learned to trust her a lot sooner than the other researchers. (*Put that in your pipe and smoke it, Peter.*)

As for bedtime, avoiding Dee in the barracks was more of a challenge – especially given how small the space was.

Rose tried going to bed earlier than everyone else. On the first night she tried it, she heard one of her bunkmates say, "She must not be used to the heat yet," and then everyone politely lowered their voices until they were ready to turn in too.

On the second night, one of them wondered if Rose was feeling sick.

And on the third night, Dee herself came over and gently shook Rose's shoulder. "Hey, you feeling okay? There's a doctor on staff if you need him."

"I'm fine," Rose said.

"You sure? Malaria's no joke. If you're sick, you should see the doctor sooner rather than later."

Rose sat up and met those stunning blue eyes, just inches from her own. She stuttered slightly as she said, "I promise, I'm fine. Thanks."

After that, she figured it was better to stay up than to worry all of her bunkmates. Anyway, the hour or so before bed when everyone settled into the barracks for the night was a great time to write down everything that had happened during the day. What was a scientist without good field notes? So Rose shifted from 'that sleepy woman' to 'the introverted one' and spent a couple of nights jotting notes, trying very hard not to let her eyes stray to Dee chatting with all the other women in the barracks, a social butterfly.

And then, on the last day of Rose's first week on the island, it happened. The kiss she never saw coming, and yet had somehow been waiting for since she first laid eyes on Dee.

It was an hour after breakfast and Rose had been observing two western Santa Cruz tortoises do nothing more exciting than dozing in the shade. It was their mating season and all the researchers were really hoping to see some nesting behavior – the species was endangered and their goal was to reverse that, if possible. But today was not the day for amorous tortoises, apparently, and Rose was feeling hot and sunburnt.

"I'm going to make a run back to the barracks for sunscreen," she told Peter, who looked bored as all get-out with his chin resting on one hand. "Can't believe I forgot it. Need anything?"

"Banana from the cafeteria?" he said.

She nodded, then headed into the jungle. That was how it felt, anyway – the paths around the research station were all lined with cacti and other wild greenery, and it was easy to imagine oneself wandering through uncharted territory. If one did not look down at the well-trodden dirt path, that is.

Rose savored the shade and the solitude. There were birds singing in the trees, and the wind rustling the leaves was a welcome relief from the heat. She was caught up in her thoughts, pondering the big questions of species preservation, when she rounded a corner and smacked right into Dee.

Their bodies collided and Rose's nose filled with Dee's familiar, earthy scent. "Oh! Sorry."

She stumbled backward and Dee put out her hands to steady her, one on each shoulder.

"Lost in your own world, huh?" Dee said, their eyes meeting now. "Better be careful with that – a panther might get you."

Rose furrowed her brow. "There are no panthers on Santa Cruz Island."

Dee laughed. "No, there aren't – I was just making sure you're lucid."

"You seem to think I'm fragile," Rose said. "The other day you thought I had malaria."

"I don't think you're fragile," Dee said. "In fact, I would guess the opposite – fiercely independent, to the point where you refuse to accept help even when you need it." She cocked an eyebrow at her. "Am I right?"

Rose reluctantly agreed. "Maybe a little."

"So, you're a strong, independent woman who's not afraid to travel across the globe to go traipsing through the jungle on her own," Dee continued. "That leaves me to wonder..."

"What?" Rose couldn't help asking.

Dee narrowed her eyes. "Have I done something to offend you?"

"Huh?"

"You've been avoiding me."

Rose's cheeks warmed, no small feat in this atmosphere. "I have not." Lying through her teeth, locking eyes with Dee and challenging her to call her out.

"You've been treating me like I'm invisible, then," Dee persisted. "Ever since that first day in the barracks. Did I embarrass you?"

"No." Rose said, although Dee's question made her remember the glob of sunscreen that had been on her nose that day.

How could she possibly explain her reason for giving Dee the cold shoulder? But she couldn't imagine a woman like this simply letting it go without an explanation.

"Scare you?" Dee guessed.

"No."

"Anger you?"

"No."

Dee took a step closer and lowered her voice. "Turn you on?"

"What?" Rose gasped, her mouth coming open with shock just as Dee let out a smirk.

"Thought so," she said, then took another step forward and hooked one hand behind Rose's head, tilting her face up so that Dee could bend down and plant a deep, soulful kiss on her lips.

Rose went rigid with shock, and then her body betrayed her, sinking into the kiss. It *was* what she wanted, and Dee had read her mind. Even better, inexplicably, it turned out she wanted the same thing. Rose tentatively let her hands rest on Dee's hips, her tongue entering the no man's land between their lips. Dee's met hers there eagerly, setting off fireworks of pleasure not only on Rose's tongue but deep in her core too.

Then, somewhere in the back of her consciousness, Rose heard the crunch of dry dirt underfoot. Someone was coming down the path and she and Dee both took a step away from each other.

One of the full-time staff members came around the bend, nodded hello to them both, then went on his way. Rose looked at Dee, her cheeks feeling just as flushed as before.

"Why did you kiss me?" she whispered.

"Because I knew you wanted me to," Dee said. "And because I wanted to, from the moment I saw you. Will you stop ignoring me now?"

"We can't do that again," Rose objected.

"Why not?"

She opened her mouth, then closed it. Yeah, *why not?* She'd come halfway around the world, spent every dollar she had to her name on this trip. She was already doing something women weren't supposed to be able to do, in a field no one particularly wanted her to be in. She was doing so many impossible things this summer... what was one more?

"I can't let it interfere with my work," she objected.

Dee nodded. "It won't, I promise." She leaned in and kissed Rose's cheek, and said, "Until next time, then. Tell any panthers you run into that you're mine now."

She turned and marched off down the path, and a shiver of desire stronger than Rose had ever felt before worked its way through her. Who *was* that presumptuous woman and why did her words turn Rose's legs into jelly?

And most importantly... when exactly was 'next time'?

10

LAUREN

Grace's friends, a couple named Marley and Blake, came back after puppy playtime was over to bring the dogs back to their training school, and Lauren helped them load the puppies into the van they brought. It had *Good Boys and Girls Academy* written on the side, with a graphic of a very eager-looking service dig at the ready.

"Thanks so much for sharing your puppies with us," Lauren said. "My residents loved the event and hopefully you can come back."

"They're not ours," Marley explained. "I'm sure if I tried to train a guide dog, it'd end up being the service animal equivalent of a foster fail."

"I can vouch for that," Blaire said, hooking her thumb at Marley. "This one's a huge sucker for anything with four paws and fur. We've got a beagle named Rainbow at home and he's enough of a handful already."

"The owner of the guide dog school, Erin, is a mutual

friend of ours from college," Marley explained. "We're just doing her a favor playing puppy chauffeur."

"I called Erin to set this up and she loved the idea of having your residents help socialize the puppies," Grace explained, "but she was already booked with a client today."

"Honestly, being a puppy chauffeur has been the highlight of my day," Blaire said. "I don't mind a bit."

"Just make sure you return the same number we borrowed or I'll be the one who hears about it," Grace joked.

Marley and Blaire closed up the van and hopped in, and Lauren noticed Grace's truck in the parking spot beside it. "You drove separate?"

"Yeah, I find it's best," she said. "Part of my job includes the glamorous task of checking for accidents and cleaning up kibble crumbs, and it's easier if the animals have already gone home at that point."

"Well, I've got some time before my next meeting," Lauren said. "I'll help you clean."

"You don't have to do that," Grace said, then she smiled, her eyes flitting down to Lauren's mouth. "But I won't say no to spending a little more time with you."

Lauren couldn't help returning the smile, even though she knew she was playing a dangerous game, mixing business with a fast-developing crush. They watched the van pull out of the parking lot, then headed back inside.

"That was really great," Lauren said while they walked. "Nobody can resist a cute puppy, and yet I was mostly watching you – you did an amazing job of pairing everybody up with the perfect puppy for their personality, and you just met my residents."

"Well, it *is* my job," Grace said, pretending to brush dirt off her shoulder.

"And you're very good at it," Lauren said. "I hope we can have you and the puppies back."

"I'd love to come back," Grace said. "However often you want me."

Lauren averted her gaze. When she called Grace to schedule today's event, she left out the part about calling Gary first and being shot down. Grace had been too excited about setting up puppy playtime, and it didn't come up.

"I'll let you know," was all she said now. "Anyway, I was really impressed with you."

Grace looked sidelong at her as they walked, a teasing smile on her face. "Yeah, I'm impressive… I know."

"You are," Lauren said, bumping her shoulder. "Modest, too."

When they got back inside, the common room was cleared out, with the exception of a few piles of abandoned kibble here and there and a couple puppy toys that had gotten kicked under chairs and overlooked.

"I'll take those back to Erin the next time I see her," Grace said, putting them in a pile near the door. "You really don't need to help me clean up – I brought my own Dirt Devil and everything."

"Well, maybe I'll just enjoy the view, then," Lauren said, locking eyes with Grace. Lord, what had gotten into her? When was the last time she was so forward with a woman, let alone one she knew she shouldn't be getting involved with?

Something about Grace's soft, dark skin and those striking, smoky eyes just scrambled her brain whenever the two of them were in the same room.

She watched Grace pick up kibble for a minute, smiling when Grace intentionally turned her back to Lauren before bending over.

"How's that view?"

Grace was wearing tight jeans and a polo shirt with her company's logo embroidered on the pocket. Not that Lauren could see her pocket right now... her eyes were definitely elsewhere. "It's a great view... unfortunately, I'm not the type to sit around and let other people do the hard work. I'll get a broom."

She pushed off the table she'd been leaning against and made a quick trip down the hall to a janitorial closet. She came back with a broom and an upright vacuum, and the two of them spent the next half-hour cleaning up the common room. While they worked, Lauren asked Grace more about her background, and Grace told her about starting out as a veterinary school student.

"That's how I met Marley, and a lot of my other friends who let me borrow their animals," she explained. "Marley has a vet clinic downtown, and Sonic's human, Syd, does wildlife rehab all around the county."

She unplugged the vacuum, done with the task.

"What about you?" Grace asked. "I started out

wanting to be a vet and wound up doing this. Did you always plan to be an assisted living facility director?"

"Not specifically," Lauren said. "Growing up, my mom was diabetic and my sister had asthma. My dad wasn't around, and they both got diagnosed within a couple months of each other. That made for some really hectic times. I helped out as best I could, and a lot of the time that meant scheduling appointments and playing chauffeur once I was old enough to drive."

"That must have been stressful," Grace frowned.

"It was, but it turned out I was pretty good at managing their care," Lauren said. "And it felt nice to be useful. I never had the stomach for nursing and I couldn't wrap my head around the student loans for medical school, so I got a degree in health administration. Imagined myself in a hospital setting, but there were so many more elder care job openings, so I wound up here."

"You seem like you enjoy your work," Grace observed.

"I love it," Lauren said. "Now that I'm here, I can't imagine working anywhere else." She laughed, thinking of Opal, who'd made a valiant attempt to shove a ten-pound puppy into a five-pound knitting bag at the end of today's activity. "It does have its challenges, though."

"As long as you feel like you've made a difference at the end of the day, that's all that matters," Grace said, then shoved her hands in her pockets. "That's what I think, anyway."

With her hands at her hips and her shoulders

hunched as a result, she looked bashful – an unusual attitude for her that charmed Lauren all the more.

Suddenly, she found herself blurting out something she hadn't intended to say. "I *may* not have gotten permission from corporate for you to come today."

Grace looked at her with an expression that was equal parts confusion and intrigue. "What?"

"In fact, I was expressly told not to work with you," Lauren added. "But you're right – what really matters is making a difference in the lives of the people, and the animals, that we care for. And it's not my fault that Gary in his corporate silo can't remember that anymore... or maybe never knew it."

Grace was grinning now. "You know, that makes sense – I was wondering how you managed to change Gary's mind so quick. Still... you disobeyed Gary for me?"

Lauren laughed. "Well, for my residents."

Grace wagged a finger at her. "I suspected you were a badass, Miss Carpenter. You've just confirmed it."

"I've just opened both of us up to a potential lawsuit," Lauren pointed out. "You should be angry at me."

Grace just shrugged. "If it comes to it, I'll deny this conversation ever happened."

"That... could work," Lauren said. "Guess I'm the only one in hot water."

"But you did it so you could see me," Grace teased. "That's sweet."

Lauren found Grace grinning. "And for my residents," she insisted.

She looked around the room – they were done cleaning and the space looked like it'd never had a dozen puppies tromping through it. Lauren gathered the cleaning supplies to return to the closet, and they both paused at the door to the common room.

"So, now that you're a rulebreaker," Grace said, "do you feel like breaking one more?"

Lauren's pulse sped up as she tried to anticipate what Grace was about to suggest. She shouldn't have given her the impression that she was a wild child. The truth was that going against Gary's wishes to schedule Grace today had damn near given her a heart attack.

"Which rule?" she asked.

"The one about not mixing business with pleasure," Grace said.

She stepped a little closer, after making sure there was no one in the hall to observe them, and ran her fingers down the lapel of Lauren's blazer. She could feel Grace's knuckle against her breastbone, and it made her whole body feel feverish.

"Cards on the table... I can't stop thinking about you, Lauren," Grace said. "I'd love to take you out sometime – sans PowerPoint slides. And I know it'd be a conflict of interest since we're working together now, but as far as your boss is concerned, I'm not even here, right?"

"I've never had someone come right out and tell me they're interested in me before," Lauren admitted. "It's always a big guessing game."

"That's a damn shame, because I think you're one of

the most interesting women I've ever met," Grace answered. "But I find it's best to be direct... Did it work?"

Lauren knew her answer should be no – she hadn't even been at this job a full year and she'd already taken a very big risk for this woman. She should be running in the opposite direction for the sake of her career – and for her health, because every time she stood so close to Grace, she forgot to breathe.

"Yes," she said. "It did work, but you better take me out quick before I come back to my senses."

Grace grinned. "What's your Saturday look like?"

"Wide open," Lauren said, the blood rushing to her head. God, she really wasn't used to living life *on the edge* like this.

"Great, I'll pick you up at eleven a.m.," Grace said. "Do you still have my number?" Lauren nodded, and Grace added, "Text me your address."

"Okay..." Grace scooped up the forgotten puppy toys and headed into the hallway. Lauren called after her, "Where are we going?"

Grace turned around, taking a couple of backwards steps, the very definition of cool as she said, "Someplace special. Dress casual, though."

11
GRACE

On Saturday morning, Grace showed up at Lauren's house promptly at eleven. She lived in a quaint little bungalow with a wide front porch in a suburb outside of Granville, which happened to be on the opposite side of town from their destination.

Lauren came skipping down off the porch before Grace had a chance to come knock on her door, but it did give her a good opportunity to drink the woman in.

She was wearing a chambray shirtdress that cinched in at her waist and drew attention to her hips, along with a pair of simple white sneakers and a wide-brimmed hat. Casual or all buttoned up in her work suits, she was positively delicious either way. Grace managed to rein in her drool before Lauren met her at her truck.

"Good morning, am I dressed appropriately?" she asked.

"You look great," Grace said. "That's perfect."

"Fooooor?" Lauren teased.

Grace laughed. "The zoo... that okay?"

"Yeah, I haven't been in ages," Lauren said. "Probably since I was a kid."

Grace let out a breath as she opened Lauren's door for her and then hopped in beside her. Zoos, and the Granville Zoo in particular, were some of her favorite places in the world, and given how much Lauren had loved the puppies and the bunny yoga and Sonic, she guessed Lauren would appreciate the zoo too.

But they got a bad rap at times, from people who didn't think the animals should be caged or due to facilities that didn't take care of their animals properly. The Granville Zoo wasn't like that – Grace knew several of the zookeepers and she had it on good authority that all the animals there were well-cared-for and better off than they would have been in the wild.

Still, the date idea was a gamble, and she was relieved that it hadn't gone over like a lead balloon.

"Why the zoo?" Lauren asked as she let Grace open her car door for her.

"It's one of my favorite places," Grace explained. "Plus, I know some of the employees and I talked them into hooking us up with a couple of private encounters."

"Sounds naughty," Lauren said, and Grace laughed.

"What I mean is we're gonna get to feed penguins," she said, smacking Lauren's knee with the back of her hand as she got into the driver's seat. "Get your mind out of the gutter, woman!"

Lauren captured Grace's hand, threading her fingers into it and keeping it on top of her bare thigh as Grace put the truck in gear. "I'm glad you asked me out. I'll be honest, I never would have made the first move as long as we had a professional relationship... but if you're willing to be unprofessional, so am I."

Grace laughed again. "My pleasure."

The zoo was busy when they arrived. Warm weather was here to stay for the season and there were families with children of all ages out taking advantage of the sunshine. Grace and Lauren wandered around to whatever exhibits struck their fancy for a little while, and Grace enjoyed watching Lauren's eyes light up just like the little kids around them.

"Everybody else was excited about the lions and the giraffes and the elephants when I went to the zoo as a kid," she explained as they wandered through the warm and humid reptile house. "Give me a gila monster any day and I'm happy."

She was looking at one through a pane of glass. The orange and black lizard was stretched out on a rock, soaking up the warmth, and it did look kinda cute in an oblivious reptile kind of way. Grace put one hand gently against the small of Lauren's back while they watched it.

"Have you ever actually been in the same room with a gila monster?" she asked. "Because I have to question just how happy you'd be once it started hissing and lunging at you. You know they're venomous, right?"

"Yeah," Lauren said, "big lizards are cool, though. Like modern dinosaurs."

"Well, next time I'll see if I can arrange for you to hold a savannah monitor," Grace promised. Then she checked her watch. "You ready to feed some penguins their lunch?"

"Heck yes," Lauren said, waving goodbye to her new gila monster friend.

Grace kept her arm wrapped around Lauren's waist as they walked, and Lauren leaned into her. "I'm so glad you're having a good time," Grace said. "This place always takes me back to my childhood – my dad used to bring me here nearly every weekend in the summers."

"Was he an animal lover too, or did he just know you were?"

"Oh, the biggest," Grace said. "He was an electrician by trade, but I think if he could have had any job in the world, it definitely would have been with animals. That's part of the reason I went to vet school – I wanted it for myself, but I also wanted to do it for him, for the dream he never got to live out. Granted, I ended up switching to a different program, but that wasn't until after he passed."

"Sounds like you two were very close," Lauren said, and Grace felt her chest tighten. She wondered why the hell she was having this conversation on their very first date.

"Not as close as I wish we were," she said. "You always wish you had more time after they're gone."

"I'm sorry." Lauren snuggled a little tighter against Grace's side as they walked. "My dad's gone too, but it's not like I even really knew him growing up. My sister and I got news a few years back that he passed, and it didn't even feel like anything had changed."

"Do you regret not having the opportunity to get to

know him more?" Grace asked. She was thinking about her own dad, about all the things she wished she'd done with him, said to him.

"Not really," Lauren said. "I hope that doesn't sound cold – it's just that he made his choice back when my sister and I were just kids. He didn't want to know us, so I promised myself I'd never spend any time pining over my lack of a father. I had a great mom, though. Still do."

"Me too," Grace said.

They walked in silence for a minute, and the penguin exhibit appeared around a corner. Grace released Lauren's waist and took her hand instead.

"Sorry about the turn that conversation just took," she said. "I didn't mean to bring up sad subjects."

Lauren shrugged. "My dad lost the power to affect me a long time ago, but it sounds like yours was a big influence in your life. I wouldn't mind hearing more about him if you want to keep talking."

Grace smiled. She *did* want to talk about him. She hadn't really processed her feelings since his death – but that was a discussion for a therapist's office, not her first date with a drop-dead gorgeous woman.

"I will tell you about him someday," she promised. "He was a great guy, and I've basically dedicated my career to him. But right now, we've got an appointment with some emperor penguins."

She pulled open the door for Lauren, and a blast of cool air greeted them, along with the squawks of happy penguins.

The date went well.

More than well, actually. After their penguin encounter, and an opportunity to feed the giraffes which Lauren passed off to a couple of kids standing nearby and looking jealous, they spent the rest of the afternoon just wandering around together.

They visited every single exhibit at the zoo, and circled back to the reptile enclosure for one more look at the gila monster. They had a late lunch from a food cart – delicious junk food that tasted like heaven after hours hiking around the zoo. And when they finally got in Grace's truck, she was still looking for things for them to do to avoid dropping Lauren off and ending their date.

They wound up at the Perky Bean, a coffee shop on the outskirts of Granville University's campus that Grace and her friends frequented when they were students. It was still some of the best coffee in town, and Lauren had never been there.

They strolled around campus for a while, getting to know each other, and from the eager way Lauren agreed to every extension of their date, Grace figured she didn't want it to end, either.

At last, though, it got dark and the temperature dropped, and Lauren said apologetically, "I should go home. I have an early conference call with Gary tomorrow and I still haven't updated the spreadsheets I'll need for it – Gary's been known to crucify people for presenting him old data."

"Seriously?" Grace asked.

"I wish I was kidding," Lauren answered.

"But tomorrow's Sunday."

Lauren just shrugged. "Meaningless to the likes of Gary. At least I can take the call from home on my laptop, in the comfort of my jammies."

"Gary seriously needs to learn some boundaries," Grace said. "And this is the same guy whose back you went behind to get me into Sunnyside?"

Lauren smiled and bumped Grace's hip with her own. "I guess you were right – I like having you around."

They kissed then. They were standing alone on the sidewalk, beneath a huge oak that had probably been growing for hundreds of years. It was dark, and the tree provided a little extra privacy for Grace and Lauren to sink into the kiss as deeply as they liked.

Grace wouldn't have minded never coming back up for air.

Eventually, though, practicality and public decency dictated they must. So she drove Lauren home, kissed her again passionately at her door, and made Lauren promise to go out with her again soon. And then she let her go.

---

*O*n Monday morning, Grace was heading to the outskirts of Granville to deliver a pair of hamsters to an elder care facility she'd been working with. She'd spent the whole rest of the weekend in a fog that smelled like Lauren's perfume. She couldn't get the dark-haired beauty out of her mind and it was as if she'd actually inhaled the woman into her body, her soul, when they kissed.

Grace had kissed her fair share of women in her life. None of them held a candle to Lauren. None of them had the power to make her heart race like Lauren did.

Why?

It was far more than her beauty, although merely being in the same room with her made Grace's core heat up. It was her compassion for the residents at Sunnyside, and the fact that she'd given up her spot in the giraffe feeding queue to a couple of kids she didn't even know, and above all, the knowledge that she'd risked her job just to see Grace again. Who could resist a woman who'd go to such lengths for them?

Grace was distracted with thoughts of their zoo date, and plans for their next one, when she arrived at Granville Estates around ten. This was a privately owned facility and a small one at that. There were only about thirty residents in the building, a homey-looking colonial that had been renovated to contain multiple studio-style suites as well as the medical facilities required.

Grace had approached the facilities director here about the same time she'd reached out to Lauren, and it'd been much easier to establish a presence here than at Sunnyside. At the Estates, the director had much more control and only needed to consult the owner and the residents when making changes. And when Grace suggested a community pet, the answer had been overwhelmingly positive.

She parked near the entrance and carefully lifted a travel cage out of her passenger seat. Inside were two winter white dwarf hamsters – one was white and the other, in spite of his name, was light brown with a dark stripe down the center of his back.

The residents and staff of the Estates had decided that hamsters were the perfect balance of cute and fluffy but low-maintenance, and Grace laughed when she got to the front entrance and noticed the banner hanging above the door. It said "Welcome Ham & Eggs" with artfully drawn depictions of both hamsters, along with their breakfast food namesakes.

She went inside and headed for the common room the hamsters would now call home. There were a ton of people waiting there – most of the residents, by Grace's estimation, as well as the staff. She lifted the travel cage up like Rafiki presenting Simba to the herd. "Ham and Eggs are here!"

People clapped, and a resident who reminded Grace of Opal over at Sunnyside came right over to take the cage out of her hands. "Can I let them out?"

"You might want to let them get acclimated for a while first, Doris," Grace recommended. "They've had an epic journey, as far as hamsters are concerned."

"Yeah, we didn't run right over and start grabbing at you when you got here," one of the other residents said, to which Doris winked.

"Wish you had, big boy," she said, which got a couple of hoots out of the other residents, and a number of rolled eyes.

A pair of staff members helped Grace bring in the rest of the hamster supplies from her truck, and they spent a couple of hours setting up a large habitat, many clear plastic tubes and tunnels, and a treat station that would dispense hamster snacks on a timer to make sure Ham and Eggs didn't get overfed by every person who walked by them.

"I still get to feed them though, right?" Doris wanted to know. She'd been looking over Grace's shoulder the whole time they were working, and she did her best to help despite a tremor in both hands.

"Of course," Grace said. She pointed to the dish where the treats would be dispensed, located on the table next to the habitat. "If the bowl's empty, you know someone recently gave them a treat. If there's one in there, that means it's been a while and you can feel free to feed them."

"So basically it's a treat dispenser for us, not the hamsters," she said.

"Yeah, I guess, though I wouldn't recommend eating these," Grace said, filling up the dispenser with dime-sized nut-and-seed balls. She set the timer, then dropped one into the dish. "Do you want to do the honors with the inaugural treat?"

"Love to," Doris said. She dropped the treat into the habitat right next to the all-white hamster, but he was too nervous about his new environment to eat. "Aww, come on, Eggs. It's good!"

"He'll eat once he gets comfortable," Grace promised.

She stayed at the Estates for the rest of the morning,

making sure everyone knew the rules of hamster care. Most of the residents were very invested in the process, and one of them – a type A personality that Grace recognized well – even took notes about everything she was telling them.

It was exactly the kind of outcome that she was hoping for, and that she desperately wanted to bring to Sunnyside and every other assisted living facility in the area. She could actually *see* the transformation taking place in the residents – if something as simple as a pair of hamsters could bring the light back into their eyes, there was no reason not to bring animals into these facilities.

She was sitting in a chair to the right of the habitat, watching the residents as they watched the hamsters, when Doris asked, "Can we hold them yet?"

It'd only been a couple of hours. Ideally, they'd wait a whole day and really give the hamsters a good chance to acclimate. But Grace could see the glimmer of excitement in the woman's eyes, and she wasn't the only one.

"Okay," she relented. "Come sit here, just in case Ham and Eggs decide to jump for it – they won't have as far to fall."

"You just think I'm going to drop him because I have the shakes," Doris accused, but with a smile.

Grace gave up her chair, and Doris plopped into it. She held out her hands and Grace went to the habitat, efficiently nabbing one of the hamsters before they had a chance to scurry into one of the many hiding places and tunnels. It was Ham, and he was breathing a little heavily in her palm, but he looked more curious than freaked out.

"Hold him firmly so he doesn't get away, but don't squeeze," she instructed as she let the hamster crawl from her palm into Doris's.

The elderly woman let out a shriek of joy, a broad smile taking over her face. "Hi, Ham, oh, I love you already!"

She brought him up to her face, a shaky journey akin to being in a paint mixer thanks to her tremor. Ham didn't seem to mind, though, and he bumped his nose into hers in exploration.

"Can I hold Eggs?" another resident asked, and Grace dipped her hand back into the habitat for the all-white hammie.

Her attention was divided between two sets of residents as they gathered around both hamsters, and then there was the part of her mind that was still on Lauren. Some of her was being professional, strategizing which type of animal might be best for Sunnyside, but most of her Lauren-related thoughts were about less noble things. Like how cute her ass looked in that shirtdress, and how delicious her lips had been. How much she wished Lauren had asked her to come in at the end of the date...

And then it happened.

Ham made a flying leap for freedom and Doris lunged to catch him, shouting. Grace whipped her head around just in time to see several sets of hands all grabbing for an airborne hamster, all of them missing by a mile. Ham landed on the carpet and now it was Grace's turn to lunge – she practically dove to the floor and cupped her hands around him before anyone panicked and flattened the little guy.

"Do you have him?" the facilities manager asked.

"I've got him," Grace said. She scooped the frightened hamster into her hands and she could feel his heart racing much harder than before. "He's okay, but that's probably enough excitement for the time being."

She got up, a little shaky as she tried to transition from lying on her belly to standing with a hamster in her hands. Apparently, Ham had had enough paint-mixing for one day and he let his dissatisfaction be known.

"Ouch!" Grace hissed, struggling not to drop him when he sank his teeth into the meaty part of her palm.

"What?" Doris asked.

"He bit me," Grace admitted, dropping Ham back into his habitat, where he immediately took refuge in a tunnel. She inspected her hand, which was bleeding. "It's okay – he was just scared. He'll be fine once he gets used to being around so many people."

"You need a bandage," the director said.

"I can patch her up," a nearby woman in scrubs said.

"Okay, thanks." Grace followed the nurse out of the common room and down the hall to a medical supply closet. Her palm throbbed and she watched the blood bead at the base of her thumb.

"He got you good," the woman said, looking at the wound when she came back out of the closet with antiseptic and bandages.

"For being such little creatures, hamsters have impressive jaw strength and sharp teeth," Grace said.

"But don't worry – they're not aggressive animals. Ham was just scared."

The woman waved her further down the hall. "I'm Annie, by the way," she said as she pointed to a chair at the nurses' station.

Grace sat down. "Nice to meet you."

Annie sat next to her and took her hand, setting it on the counter so she could disinfect the wound and bandage her up. She was sitting a little closer than necessary, and she kept stealing looks at Grace. Her interest was clear, and Grace couldn't help being flattered – Annie was pretty, the type of woman Grace might have asked out in the past. But right now? She only had eyes for Lauren.

Grace left the nurses' station a couple minutes later all patched up, leaving a slightly disappointed woman in her wake.

Was it out of character for her to be a one-woman kind of girl? Definitely.

But did she also have a damn near constant urge to call Lauren, ask her out to dinner, and tell her all about her day? Yes, ma'am.

12
LAUREN

That evening, Lauren got to hear all about the saga of Ham and Eggs over dinner at a chic little Italian bistro. In turn, Lauren told Grace about Opal's latest attempt at entertaining the other residents – she'd spent the better part of the afternoon distributing liquid chalk markers and encouraging people to paint murals on all the windows of the facility.

"Where did she even get those markers?" Grace asked.

"'Alexa, order me window markers,'" Lauren quoted. "I swear, voice-command online shopping is the worst thing to happen to elder care in a long time. But everybody had fun, and some of our residents are surprisingly artistic. I'm gonna have to schedule a painting class or something."

They talked about how much the Granville Estates residents loved their new hamsters, and over decaf and dessert, Grace pointed out that if it weren't for stick-in-the-mud Gary, Sunnyside could have a pair of adorable furry residents too.

"I know today was only the first day, but you should have seen how happy everyone was," she said. "It's going really well."

"So well that you got bit," Lauren retorted, gesturing to the bandage over Grace's fingertip. "I'm already questioning what the heck I was thinking bringing puppies in. I can only imagine Gary will make it out to be World War III if someone gets bit."

"No one will get bit," Grace reassured her. "I knew better than to let people handle the hamsters on their very first day. They were uncomfortable, but I wanted the residents to be happy so I did it anyway. *That's* why I got bit."

"Well, Sunnyside is not ready for hamsters, that's for sure," Lauren said. "What am I supposed to do with them every time Gary shows up? Hide them in a closet?"

Grace laughed. "You could have some nice, quiet animals. I noticed how much you loved that lop at Parker's rescue."

"Don't you dare," Lauren laughed. "I'd rather not lose my job."

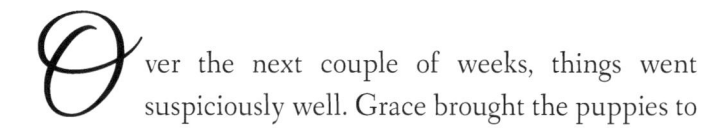

Over the next couple of weeks, things went suspiciously well. Grace brought the puppies to

Sunnyside a couple more times and Gary was none the wiser, and Lauren's worries slowly evaporated.

They went out as often as they could in the evenings – whenever Lauren wasn't putting out fires at work. Sometimes they kept things casual, meeting up for dinner or a romantic walk in the twilight. Other dates were planned in advance, like their trip to the natural history museum and the time they ventured to the Rainbow Room for drinks and dancing.

Grace was a stunningly attractive woman, and Lauren's cheeks always hurt after their dates from smiling so much. It all felt so right... and yet a part of her held back.

Every time a date ended, they sealed it with a kiss. Fiery, deep, delicious kisses, much too passionate for Lauren's front porch. And yet she resisted the urge to invite Grace inside. As much as she wanted to take the next step – as much as she wanted Grace – she just couldn't do it.

She didn't have the time to dedicate to a full-blown relationship. Half the time, their plans got postponed because she ended up working late or returning to Sunnyside after she'd left for the day. And she still couldn't fully silence the little voice in her head that said getting involved with Grace was a bad idea – how would it reflect on both of them if Gary did find out what they were doing with the puppies, and that they were dating on top of that?

Lauren was a good girl. She followed the rules, and

one of them was that you don't mix business and pleasure. Especially if it was likely to get you fired or worse.

Not that Grace was easy to resist.

Those smoky eyes. That long, lean body. The way she casually draped her arm around Lauren's shoulder or snaked it around her waist when they walked. The feel of her brushing teasingly, tauntingly against Lauren's body on the dance floor at the Rainbow Room.

On more than one occasion, when the date ended and Lauren regretfully left Grace on the porch, she'd gone straight to her bedroom and retrieved her favorite vibrator from her bedside drawer. It was a welcome relief, but she knew it was a pale imitation compared to what it would be like to really surrender herself to Grace.

She had her residents to think of, though. It was her job to keep their best interests at heart, and that meant maintaining some small semblance of restraint, of separation between her work and her private life. What little of it there was.

One day about a month after Grace had come into her life, they were grabbing a quick lunch at the Perky Bean. Grace had a bunny yoga session scheduled that evening, so they were getting their fill of each other in the middle of the day.

While Lauren bit into the panini she'd ordered, Grace pulled a stack of papers out of her satchel and set them on the table. "I found something interesting yesterday."

"What is it?" Lauren asked, cheeks full.

"An article from the *Journal of Aging and Health*," Grace said. "There's a nursing home in Tennessee that got every resident who wanted one a canary, and the outcomes have been stellar. Morale is way up, the residents have really bonded with their birds and appreciated the responsibility of caring for them, and the staff have even reported that a lot of the residents are more independent than before."

"Really?" Lauren set down her sandwich and picked up the article. "That's amazing."

"It really is." While Lauren skimmed, Grace kept talking, excited. "Ham and Eggs are doing really well over at the Estates, but they're in a common area and they don't belong to anyone in particular. There's no individual sense of responsibility. This, though–"

Lauren looked at her, a skeptical eyebrow raised. "What are you getting at?"

"Don't you think it'd be amazing if your residents could do this someday?" she said. "The ones that have their own fully appointed suites with everything they'd need to take care of them–"

"Grace."

"–and you know how bad Opal wants her own pet," she went on. "She tries to steal a puppy every time I bring them–"

"*Grace,*" Lauren interrupted, setting the article down. She took Grace's hand, rubbing her thumb gently over the scabbed over spot where Ham bit her. "Dozens of canaries in a building that's not supposed to have any animals at all? I'm already pushing my luck with the puppies... that would be nuts."

"I'm not talking about doing this tomorrow, and it doesn't have to be birds," Grace said. "We can find something small, quiet, and easy to care for – like the hamsters. We could even do different animals based on the residents' preferences. Opal would clearly love a cat, and I've heard Dee talking about turtles on multiple occasions."

"Rodent poop, salmonella, that parasite cats carry in their feces that gets into your brain," Lauren said, giving Grace a sympathetic smile. "I'm just anticipating Gary's objections – assuming he bothers to list them and doesn't just have me escorted from the building."

Grace just smiled back at her.

"What?" Lauren asked, slightly frustrated.

"I'm falling for you," Grace said, that soft smile on her lips, simple as that.

A jolt of surprise shot through Lauren. Where had that come from? They were talking about companion animals! And yet, it wasn't the bad kind of jolt – in fact, it felt pretty damn good.

"You are?" Inside, her mind was already busy protesting. *She is? Neither of us should be thinking like that... it's only going to end poorly, when I get too busy to keep this up, when I ghost her like everyone else and spoil our professional relationship in the process.*

And yet, there was another thought running beneath the others.

I think I'm falling for her too.

"Yes," Grace said, reaching across the café table and taking her hand. "And I think you feel the same."

Lauren blushed at her forwardness. She looked away.

We can't do this. We'll both get hurt. She offered up a weak excuse. "I mean, you're very compassionate, about the animals as well as the people you help. I love spending time with you, and the work you do is inspiring."

When she finally willed herself to meet Grace's gaze again, she found her grinning. "Nah, you're not falling for me in a professional capacity. You *like* me."

And who wouldn't, with that megawatt smile and the way her eyes drew Lauren into them? Lauren let out a sigh. "Maybe," she said. "But I really shouldn't like you like that."

"Why not?" Grace challenged.

"It's dangerous," Lauren breathed.

Grace narrowed her eyes. "Danger can be a good thing sometimes – exciting."

Lauren was still vibrating from that conversation when she got back to her office after lunch and found her phone blinking with multiple new voicemails. According to the caller ID, they were all from Gary.

"Shit," she said, her good mood slipping away as she sank down in her chair. No matter what Gary wanted, if he bothered to pick up the phone instead of just emailing her, it was guaranteed to give her a headache. She put the phone on speaker and listened to the first message.

"Lauren, it's Gary, we need to talk," he said, his voice curt and clipped. "Call me back."

Well, that could be anything. An order without any context was nothing new, but two more messages awaited her, and Gary wasn't normally this impatient. She advanced to the next one.

"I'm very unhappy about some rumors I've heard about your facility and I think you better call me back as soon as you can so we can clear them up," he said, then there was the click of him disconnecting the call.

Lauren's panini was suddenly settling in her stomach like a stone, and she didn't even bother with the third voicemail. She just picked up the receiver and dialed Gary's extension. Rumors? What could they possibly be about but the puppies?

"Lauren," Gary barked in her ear the second he picked up the phone. "So glad you found the time to return my call."

"I was at lunch," Lauren said. *Am I not permitted to take breaks anymore?* She wondered, but held her words back. She knew she was in trouble – now was not the time to argue.

"Well, I have concerns," Gary said. Then he paused, waiting for the air to fill with the proper amount of dread. And it did.

"Concerns, Mr. Peterson?"

"I was informed that you've been bringing that woman with the fox into the facility against my express orders not to," he said. No more messing around, building up tension. It was time for the verbal smackdown.

Lauren took a deep breath. "Her name is Grace Williams, and you said she could not bring the fox due to the risk of Lyme disease. She's been bringing service dogs, all of whom are in perfect health."

That was a stretch of the truth – Lauren knew damn well Gary's refusal had been categorical. Just trying to squeeze through that loophole made her break into a flop sweat, but she always knew this moment would come. It was time to mount her defense, loaded up with all the data Grace had given her.

"You know I meant no to the entire idea," Gary snapped.

Just who had 'informed' Gary about the puppies, anyway? Lauren hadn't received a single complaint, and so many of the residents came to puppy playtime each week. None of her employees had an ax to grind, that she knew of... in fact, she thought she'd been doing a pretty admirable job of winning everyone over in her first year here.

"With all due respect, Mr. Peterson, you're not here on a daily basis," Lauren said, surprising herself by spontaneously growing a backbone. "You haven't seen the benefits of Grace's program. The residents are so much happier, and quantitatively, there are studies I can show you–"

"Enough," Gary said. "You're right, I'm not at the facility every day, but *you* have no experience at the corporate level. What do you think would happen to the entire Sunnyside network if your gross negligence results in a lawsuit that closes the whole company down? How many of our residents all over the state will be out on the street thanks to you?"

Gross negligence? We're talking about golden retriever puppies, for fuck's sake. Lauren managed to bite back her outrage and maintain her professional tone.

"I understand your concern," Lauren said in a measured voice. "But you didn't hire me to worry about the company as a whole – you hired me to make sure that our Granville residents are as well cared for as possible, which includes their emotional wellbeing. That's what I'm doing."

She heard the sharp intake of breath as Gary wound up to go another round with her, but Lauren cut him off as her indignation bubbled over after all.

"And it's not like I'm bringing vicious, untrained dogs into the building, or encouraging the residents to lick frogs I found in the pond," she said. "We're talking about puppies, future service dogs, and the residents love them. As long as I am the director here, I will continue to schedule Grace's events in the best interest of my residents. If you don't like it, you can fire me, but then you'll have an awful lot of angry residents *and* staff members. If you'd like to discuss this with the legal team and have them come up with safety guidelines for minimizing risk while still allowing the animals to be here, I'd be happy to work with them. Good afternoon, Gary."

She hung up the phone, then immediately planted both elbows on her knees in case she started hyperventilating. She'd never done anything but say 'yes, sir' and 'yes, ma'am' to every authority figure in her life, and this was one gigantic 'hell no.'

She wasn't sure she'd ever used Gary's first name while addressing him, either.

The hyperventilation didn't happen, but when Lauren sat up, feeling weak and shaky, she let her head flop against the back of her chair. *Holy shit,* she thought, and toggled her computer mouse to wake up her monitor. Would Gary email her termination notice to her right away, or would he have to run it up the chain of command first?

13
GRACE

Lauren told Grace what happened on her call via text, and filled in all the details for her when they met up the following evening. This time, Grace finally got past the front porch, so to speak. She invited Lauren over to her place for takeout and a movie. They never got to the movie.

"I can't believe you went to bat for your residents like that, and me too," Grace said as soon as she heard the whole story. "You're amazing, you know that?"

"I'm scared shitless is what I am," Lauren answered. "I don't know what got into me and I'm shocked I haven't already been fired."

"Total, unmitigated badassery," Grace said, and Lauren laughed. Grace wrapped her arms around her. "Seriously, you're my hero."

"For being totally unprofessional to my boss?" Lauren asked.

"No," Grace said. "You remember when we were at

the zoo and I told you my dad was a huge part of why I decided to go to vet school, why I do what I do?"

"Mmhmm?"

"Well, what I didn't feel was good first-date material was the fact that he died in assisted living," she said. "He had pancreatic cancer."

"I'm sorry."

"Me too," Grace said, a lump forming in the back of her throat despite her best efforts not to let it. "He made it longer than the doctors thought he would – he was a fighter. But the whole time he was dying, I was on the other side of the country. I'd landed a prestigious summer internship and I thought my education was more important than my own sick father."

"I didn't know you back then, but I find it hard to believe that's true," Lauren said, taking her hand and squeezing.

"I did tell him I'd leave the internship. He told me not to come home, he tried to downplay his illness," Grace allowed. "But I was studying medicine. Animals, not people, sure, but it doesn't take a medical doctor to know how serious pancreatic cancer is. A part of me didn't want to believe it. I wanted to think he'd be there when I got home, recovering even."

"You weren't there when he passed?" It was said with concern, but all Grace could feel was the guilt she'd carried around with her for the last two years.

Grace swallowed around the lump. She couldn't even say the word – she just shook her head *no*.

"I'm sorry," Lauren said, wrapping her arms around

Grace and pulling her head down to her shoulder. She kissed her forehead.

Grace allowed herself to be comforted for just a moment, then sat up again. "I wasn't there and I will blame myself for that for the rest of my life, but I did talk to him on the phone every chance I got, until he was too weak to hold a conversation. And one of the things he mentioned the most, other than missing me, was missing his dog, Toni. She couldn't go to the facility with him, and we couldn't afford to pay for a round-the-clock nurse so he could stay home with her. I wasn't around either, so we had to rehome her. I always thought it would have been so much easier for him if he'd at least had Toni."

"So you started your business to help people like your dad," Lauren said, and Grace nodded.

"It's the least I could do, and I don't want to get all gloomy again... I just wanted you to know why it's so important to me that you're willing to fight for this along with me," she said. "You get it."

"I do," Lauren said, and she leaned over to kiss a tear from Grace's cheek. It was the only one she'd allowed to fall, biting the rest back, but Lauren's lips against her skin stirred new emotion in her.

She captured Lauren's face in her hands, redirecting her lips to meet her own. The kiss deepened, Lauren's lips parting and Grace's tongue gliding over them. Lauren let out a low moan, and fire ignited between Grace's thighs.

She pulled back just enough to murmur against Lauren's mouth, "Thank you."

"For what?"

"Being you," she said. "Being amazing."

And then she pushed Lauren down on the couch, lowering her onto her back and lying down alongside her. The curves and the warmth of Lauren's body were divine pressed up against Grace's lithe form, and she was suddenly ravenous for something other than the Chinese takeout they'd left untouched on the coffee table.

She ran one hand up Lauren's side, enjoying the curve of her hip and the dip of her waist, stopping just shy of the bottom of her bra. Lauren bent one leg, hugging Grace with her thigh.

"Too fast?" Grace asked.

Lauren shook her head. "Just right."

Grace's fingers tripped over Lauren's underwire and her thumb brushed the swell of her breast. "More?"

"Yes," Lauren breathed. She put her hand on Grace's hip and squeezed, then pulled her close, until they were both turned sideways, towards each other on the couch, and their hips touched. "You feel so good."

"So do you," Grace said, palm cupping Lauren's breast. She could feel the nipple pebbling against her hand, even through two layers of fabric. Her own body was vibrating with need.

They explored each other slowly, savoring every inch as the moment finally came. Their hands found every nook and curve of each other's bodies, snaking beneath fabric and stripping away the layers until there was nothing between them. Grace could feel Lauren's wetness against her thigh, and those hard little nipples poked her own chest, sending shivers through her.

"Bedroom?" she asked at last, when they'd done everything they could on a narrow couch and she was panting with lust, ready to come at the mere suggestion of a touch.

"Point the way," Lauren said, nodding eagerly.

Grace got up, stark naked and glad that summer had finally come. The air in her apartment was warm and comfortable, and she couldn't wait to throw the covers off her bed and make love to Lauren, see her spread-eagle and bared to the world – or at least to Grace. She held her hand out and helped Lauren to her feet, and couldn't resist pulling her into one more passionate kiss in the living room.

It morphed into something hungry, their thighs finding the crease of each other's legs, their bodies clinging together like a tsunami threatened to sweep them apart. "Go, now," Grace said, biting Lauren's lower lip and swatting her ass even as she pointed toward the bedroom.

Lauren let go, turned and sauntered away, emphasizing the sway of her hips for Grace's benefit.

"God damn, you are the most gorgeous woman who ever walked the earth," Grace said, shaking her head at her luck as she hurried to catch up. "I've been dreaming of this moment."

"Me too," Lauren said with a flirtatious look over her shoulder.

"What changed your mind?" Grace couldn't help

asking. She'd been patient, and she would have continued to wait, but she was aching for Lauren, practically drooling as she followed her down the hall.

"I guess throwing caution to the wind at work made me realize just how precarious life is," Lauren said. "There's no time to waste."

Grace grinned. "No, but we've got all the time in the world together tonight."

Lauren found the bedroom at the end of a short hall, and Grace watched her crawl onto the bed, giving her a great view of Lauren's perfectly round, plump ass. She got a running start and leaped onto the bed with Lauren, making the box springs bounce. Grace caught Lauren in her arms and flipped her onto her back, landing acrobatically with her knees straddling Lauren's hips.

They kissed again, and Grace took full advantage of Lauren's bared breasts, massaging them with both hands and memorizing the shape of her. "I want to taste you," she groaned as she slid her palms down over Lauren's ribs and to her hips.

"So do it," Lauren said, a glimmer in her eyes. She bucked her hips playfully, and Grace had to reach up and grab the headboard to keep from toppling over.

Then she lowered her mouth down to Lauren's. Their tongues entwined, and Grace arched her back, her breasts pressing needily against Lauren's body. Lauren moaned against her, and cupped Grace's ass in her hands.

"Flip over," she said. "I want to taste you too."

Grace pulled back to look at her, a wry smile on her lips. "Look who's bossy now."

"I guess telling Gary off awoke something in me," Lauren said with a smirk. "I kind of like telling people exactly what I want."

"Tell me," Grace challenged. "What do you want tonight?"

"Your thighs against my ears," Lauren said, "and your head between my legs."

Grace's clit throbbed at the idea. She gave Lauren one last, sultry kiss, then turned her body around, feet touching the headboard. She grabbed a pillow and stuffed it under Lauren's hips, then lowered her head right where Lauren wanted it.

"Like this?" she teased, letting her hot breath tickle Lauren's clit. Her sex was wet and swollen with desire, her clit already peeking out of its hood, just as eager for Grace as the rest of Lauren was.

"More," Lauren said, then wrapped her arms around Grace's hips and drew her down to meet her mouth. There was a long, wet swipe of her tongue along the whole length of Grace's pussy, and it had her thighs quaking already.

"That's fantastic," she growled, then gave up teasing and dove between Lauren's creamy thighs. She was sweet and musky, and she squirmed with pleasure every time Grace touched her.

Grace lavished attention on every inch of Lauren's sex, with her tongue and with her fingers. She made her come twice before Lauren had her so close herself that she could no longer split her attention, and then she just looped her arm around Lauren's thigh and held on for dear life as Lauren lapped and sucked at her clit.

Grace came in an explosion of ecstasy and quivering muscles, then melted down on top of Lauren, breathing hard. After a moment of blissful clinging to her, cheek to Lauren's inner thigh, she rolled off onto her back.

"Worth the wait?" Lauren asked, getting up and crawling down to the foot of the bed with Grace.

"What wait?" Grace asked back. "I was enjoying the lusty, torturous goodnight kisses." Lauren laughed and Grace mustered her strength to roll onto her side, throwing an arm possessively around Lauren's middle. "Besides, I'm far from finished with you tonight."

Lauren's termination notice never came after her call with Gary. She walked around Sunnyside holding her breath and waiting for a whole week after, but something Lauren said to the man must have gotten through his stubborn head because she didn't hear another peep from him.

A month passed quite peacefully, and Grace kept bringing the service puppies, who were all becoming very comfortable with their new human friends and getting ready to start training in earnest.

One afternoon while Lauren, Grace and the puppies' trainer Erin were loading them back into the van after playtime, Grace asked, "Did Gary ever get back to you about the lawyer stuff?"

Lauren shook her head. "Haven't heard a peep from him. Either he talked to them and they told him his concerns are totally baseless, in which case he's avoiding me because he would never admit such a thing..."

"Or?" Erin asked.

"Or he's quietly scheming my demise," Lauren said.

"I don't think he's a subtle kind of guy," Grace pointed out.

She'd tried talking to him directly, both for her own goal of expanding outside the Granville area and to take some of the heat off Lauren. She'd weaseled his phone number out of Lauren and called him, armed to the teeth with literature and statistics and defenses against his legal liability concerns. And she all she got was his voicemail.

She called back three separate times, and got sent to voicemail each time.

"Is he avoiding me or do I just have rotten timing?" she'd asked Lauren after her attempts.

"It's Gary – both might be true," Lauren had said. "Keep trying."

"Can I have his email?"

"Sure, but he barely reads them," Lauren had answered. "Try sending your data in spreadsheet format – they seem to be his weakness."

She was joking, but Grace did just that. She made her case in the body of her email, laying out her ideas for the Granville location and for the Sunnyside network as a whole. And for good measure, she also included every scrap of data she could muster in a pretty spreadsheet attachment.

And got crickets in return.

Grace wasn't the type to give up – she'd launched her business on nothing but a borrowed fennec and a couple of homemade pamphlets. But damn if Gary Peterson wasn't the strongest brick wall she'd ever come across. She now had a much better understanding of what Lauren was up against.

But he'd taken no steps to stop puppy playtime, so Lauren had decided there was no harm in continuing.

After they saw Erin and the puppies off, Lauren asked Grace if she had time for an afternoon cup of coffee. They both always had more work to do – such were the lives of a business owner and a manager – and there was no time to drive to the Perky Bean. But Grace was always looking for an excuse to linger with Lauren a bit longer, and they headed to Sunnyside's dining room for a quick cup.

"Want to sit for a couple minutes?" Lauren asked as they filled their cups from a Keurig. "I have a staff meeting scheduled, but it doesn't start for another forty-five minutes."

"I'm all yours," Grace said.

The room was empty at this time of day, and they found a table by a window that looked out on the pond. "I still never found out who told Gary about the puppies," Lauren said as their feet mingled under the table. "I have no real suspects, either."

"Nobody around here who hates puppies?" Grace teased.

"Who could hate a puppy?" Lauren wondered. "I

have to be honest, though, I'm proud of us for continuing puppy playtime because it's what's best for the residents, but I walk around here feeling like Gary's lurking around every corner, getting ready to come back on me with guns blazing at any moment."

"The fact that you yelled at him and disobeyed a direct order and he hasn't done a single thing for a whole month tells me he's all bark and no bite," Grace said. "Maybe he secretly likes the idea too, and he's just afraid to stick his own neck out there with his own higher-ups."

"Oh, he definitely has no backbone," Lauren agreed, rolling her eyes. "That's why he's so stingy with the budget. He thinks if we go a dollar over budget, he's the one who's going to get the ax."

"Well, I'll be sure to include a plan for minimizing impact on the facility budget next time I email him," Grace said.

Lauren laughed. "You're still trying?"

Grace sat up a little taller. "I don't give up when there's something I want – especially when I know how important it is for the people I care about. So, speaking of axes..."

Lauren cocked her head. "What kind of transition is that?"

"Have you heard about the ax throwing range they installed behind the bowling alley?" Grace said. "A bunch of my friends are going – they like to get together about once a month and try something new and weird. I thought you might want to come with me, meet some of them."

Lauren smiled. "You want me to meet your friends?"

"Well, you've already met Parker, Marley and Blaire," Grace said. "They'll all be there, along with a few others. They've been asking about you."

Now Lauren was grinning from ear to ear. "You've been talking to your friends about me?"

"Of course," Grace said. "You haven't done the same?"

Lauren laughed. "What friends? Unless Opal counts..."

"Okay, that does it – you're *definitely* coming ax throwing," Grace said. "You need a social life and I'm making it my mission to give it to you."

Lauren's gaze turned coy and she said, "I do like it when you *give it to me*."

"Mmm, naughty girl..."

Before Grace got the chance to expand on that thought, someone knocked on the doorframe. They turned to see Dee in the doorway. "Hey, am I interrupting?"

"Not at all," Lauren lied. "Come in. Looking for an afternoon snack?"

"No, I wanted to talk to you two, actually," Dee said. "Do you mind?"

"Have a seat," Grace said, pulling a chair out from the table for her.

Dee never missed a puppy playtime, although Grace had noticed that it seemed to have less to do with the puppies and more to do with one of the other residents. Dee always had her eye on Rose, and she tried to talk to her on the rare occasion that Rose's daughter wasn't hovering nearby. Grace got the impression that a romance was budding – or it would be if Rose's family gave it some room to grow.

It took Dee a moment to make it across the room with her cane. She favored her left leg, and Grace knew from chatting to her that she was still healing from a hip fracture. When Dee finally eased down in the chair Grace had pulled out for her, she asked, "What can we do for you?"

"Maybe nothing," Dee said. "I know I'm not supposed to be talking about other residents' private medical information... but Rose is sick, and I don't know how much time she has left. I want to do something for her before she..."

She couldn't finish the sentence, emotion welling up in her eyes. This was more than a budding romance – Dee was in love with Rose.

"What did you have in mind?" Lauren asked.

"I'm sure you don't know this – even Rose seems to have forgotten – but we knew each other, once upon a time," Dee said. "We worked together. She was a herpetology grad student and I was studying climate change, before anybody really called it that in the mainstream."

"Herpetology?" Lauren asked.

"The study of amphibians and reptiles," Grace supplied, and Dee nodded.

"She was specifically interested in giant tortoises back when I knew her, and the research she's published since then tells me she stuck with them through her career," she said. "She sits and pets the puppies... whenever her daughter will allow her to come–" Resentment bit into her voice. "–but I can tell from the look in her eyes that they're just not the same as the giant tortoises she spent her career studying."

Lauren smiled and reached out to put her hand on top of Dee's. "You want to help her reconnect with her life's work one last time, is that it?"

"Yes," Dee said. "And I must admit, on a selfish level, I hope that it will jog her memory as far as I'm concerned."

Lauren sat back and let out a sigh. "There's no way we can bring a tortoise in here – it'd be too much of a health risk. They carry salmonella, right?"

"Not to mention the fact that it's a bit harder to borrow a giant tortoise than a puppy," Grace said, and then the gears started turning. "However... I know a zoologist I could beg another favor from. Can Rose travel?"

"You want to take her to the zoo?" Lauren asked.

"If she can make the trip, I can get her into the tortoise enclosure" Grace nodded, and Dee's eyes lit up.

"You could actually get her inside?" she asked. "Not just on the other side of the glass?"

"I'll do my best," Grace promised, turning to Lauren. "If you think it's safe."

"I'll talk to Angelique to be sure," Lauren said. "She'll know all the details of Rose's medical care, but as far as I know, there's no reason she can't take a car ride. We'll be pushing her in a wheelchair the whole time, and we can keep it to a short trip."

"And I can come along?" Dee asked. The mix of hope and desperation in her eyes broke Grace's heart and she answered before Lauren even had a chance to.

"Yes, you should – it was your idea."

Relief washed over Dee's features, quickly followed by a frown. "What about her daughter? There's no way she'd allow Rose to go, and if she did, she wouldn't want me there. I don't know why, but she clearly hates me."

"I'm sure it's not personal," Lauren said. "She hates me too."

Lauren frowned, and Grace sat back. She could make sure that Rose got VIP treatment once they got her to the zoo, but all the details leading up to it were beyond her control. Lauren thought for a minute, a stern expression on her face, and Grace guessed that she was doing the same torturous mental calculations she'd done when she decided to disobey Gary.

Finally, she lowered her voice to say, "Rose's children do not have power of attorney, however, that detail does not leave this room because I am not authorized to share it."

Dee nodded.

"I would never go against a family's wishes if I thought it would harm my residents," Lauren went on. "But I've seen how Gina is with her mother, and how Rose seems to barely take a breath when she's around. So maybe it wouldn't be the worst thing in the world if the three of us make plans for a zoo excursion, and Rose decides to tag along at the last minute."

Dee was already grinning. "Thank you so much–"

"But," Lauren interrupted, her voice going sharp, "it's up to Rose. If she doesn't want to go, that's that. And this plan does not leave this room or Gary will fire me before you can say 'tortoise.'"

Dee held out her hand to shake on it. When Lauren accepted, she said, "I won't breathe a word of any of this. Thank you so much, you're the best – both of you." She shook Grace's hand for good measure, then stood up laboriously and limped her way out of the room.

When she was gone, Grace looked at Lauren. "You okay?"

"I think I'm having a heart attack," Lauren smiled. "Why did I agree to that?"

"Because you're an amazing, compassionate woman," Grace said, then reached under the table to squeeze Lauren's knee. "And it's sexy as hell watching you break the rules so people can rekindle old flames."

14
DEE

Lauren and Grace came through just as Dee had been hoping. They spent a whole week strategizing and getting all the pieces of the puzzle into place, and then on Wednesday morning, it was Dee's turn.

Rose's son was hardly ever around so he was a bit of a wildcard, but Gina had a standing work appointment every Wednesday that took up most of her day. She couldn't possibly show up to Sunnyside until the afternoon, that made it the obvious choice for Operation: Tortoise Reunion, as Dee had been thinking of it in her head.

Right after breakfast, which Rose had taken in her room as usual, Dee stepped into her open door and knocked on the frame.

Rose looked up from her recliner. It'd be real nice to see her out of that thing – Dee knew she was sick, but sitting in an overstuffed chair all day long, looking forlornly out the window, was just wallowing in it. "Yes?" Rose asked.

"I have a bit of an unusual request," Dee said. "May I come in?"

Rose gestured to the small dining table pushed up against one wall. While Dee made her way over to it, she asked, "Was that the request?"

Dee smiled. "Not quite, but it's good to see you haven't lost your sense of humor."

Rose frowned. Dee had tried several times over the last few weeks to jog Rose's memory, but she was still acting like they'd never met before. As if that summer hadn't been the most unforgettable thing Dee had ever experienced. Rose had to be faking – she had no other signs of memory loss, and Dee refused to believe that she was so forgettable. But even when it was just the two of them talking, Rose held fast.

Dee sat down, pulling the dining chair closer to Rose's recliner. "How are you feeling today?" she asked, resisting the urge to reach out and take Rose's hand.

"I've had better days," Rose said. "But I've also had worse."

"What do you think of going on a little adventure?"

A spark ignited in Rose's gaze. Good – she wasn't completely resigned to retreating inside herself and waiting out her time on this earth. "What are you talking about?" she asked.

"I know you don't remember me," Dee played along, "but you haven't forgotten your research, have you? Your life's work with the tortoises?"

"Of course not," Rose said, sitting a little taller. "I published over thirty papers."

"And I've read every one I could find," Dee couldn't resist telling her. "Your passion for your work is inspiring, and I bet it's been a while since the last time you got to be around the giant tortoises that you love. How long ago did you retire?"

"Five years," Rose said. "I would still be working if the cancer treatment hadn't taken such a toll, but in the end it forced my hand."

"Well, I'd like to do something for you, Rose," Dee said, taking her hand after all. She just couldn't help herself – this was the first time they'd been well and truly alone since Rose arrived here, and Dee refused to give up hope that she still meant something to her. "I talked to Grace, the woman who runs the puppy playtimes, and she's got a friend at the zoo who can get us into the tortoise enclosure for an hour or so. As long as you're up for it, I'd like to take you to the zoo to see them."

Rose was beaming and she squeezed Dee's hand. "When?"

"Right now," Dee said, and held her breath. Lauren said that if Rose wasn't up for it, the whole idea would crash and burn here and now. It was the best idea Dee had to break her out of her shell, and from the pallor of Rose's skin, she wasn't sure there was time for another good idea.

"Just the two of us?" Rose asked.

Dee nodded. "Well, the two of us plus Grace and Lauren."

Rose looked down at her lap. "I can't walk all the way through the zoo anymore. Getting to the dining room is too much for me most days."

"Lauren has a wheelchair waiting for you out in the hall," Dee said, then smirked to add, "and one for me as well – turns out I'm no spring chicken either and I'm not up for hobbling around the zoo with my cane."

"Okay," Rose said. "Let's go."

"Really?" Dee asked, lighting up. Before Rose had a chance to second-guess her decision, she turned toward the open door and called, "Lauren, Grace, come on in – let's get this show on the road!"

Rose laughed. "That quickly? I feel like I'm being kidnapped."

"To be perfectly honest," Lauren said as she pushed Rose's wheels for the day into the room, "we sort of feel like we're kidnapping you. Please don't take this the wrong way, but your daughter is very protective of you."

"She's just scared to lose her mom," Rose said as Lauren and Grace helped her transfer over to the wheelchair. "She had a very hard time of it when her father died."

"Losing a parent is always terrible," Grace said.

Rose smiled up at her. "I do know she's overbearing – but if it helps her cope, who am I to tell her to back off?"

"You're a good mother," Lauren said.

"I'd love to hear more about your family on the way to the zoo," Dee said as she stepped forward to take the handles of the wheelchair. She only got to push Rose out to the hall, where her own chair was waiting for her, but it felt right to be there.

They made it to the zoo by noon, and it had taken a little bit of prodding, but Rose opened up about her life in between the Galapagos and Sunnyside during the drive.

Dee now knew that Rose's parents had taken it upon themselves to find a husband for her after grad school. They'd been worried about how studious she was, and how she prioritized her career over romance.

"My mother was from the generation that believed if women went to college at all, the sole purpose was to find a man," she said. "She was horrified that I'd made it all the way through my bachelor's degree without getting married, The fact that I went on to graduate school was incomprehensible to her."

"I trained my parents pretty early on that they shouldn't expect me to get married," Dee said. "But I got the same kinds of questions from my mother. So you let her matchmake for you?"

Rose nodded. "To her credit, she knew me well – she found someone who was just as dedicated to his career as I was, and who didn't expect me to become a housewife. It worked on that level, so I kept dating him, and we got lucky – we fell in love."

Dee felt her heart clenching in her chest. She couldn't begrudge Rose the life she'd lived for the past sixty years, when they'd been apart. But the emotional side of her raged with jealousy that Rose could love anyone who wasn't her. At least it had been a man – that somehow made the knowledge sting a little less.

When Lauren pulled up in front of the zoo entrance, Dee was reminding herself that she'd slept with other women in her life, and even loved a few of them. None as deeply or frantically or profoundly as Rose, but loved them nonetheless. Maybe the same was true for Rose – she loved her husband, but not in the same way.

The two young whippersnappers of their group helped Dee and Rose into their wheelchairs, and Grace stayed with them while Lauren found a parking spot for the van they'd borrowed from Sunnyside. Then they went inside the zoo, and Rose was quiet while they made their way to the tortoise enclosure. Her eyes were wide, though, taking it all in with a smile on her face.

"This is wonderful," Dee said, enjoying the soft breeze on her face as Grace pushed her chair. "One day, we should have an outing with everyone – except Opal, of course."

Grace laughed. "Why do you hate her so much?"

"She broke my hip."

Rose gasped. "She did?"

Dee grumbled. "Well, she scared me and I fell out of bed and broke my own hip... but I would not have fallen if she wasn't there. And to this day, she's never apologized."

She looked over at Rose, gauging her reaction. She'd meant her quip about excluding Opal to be a joke, but now she just sounded hateful. That was not the version of herself she wanted to present to Rose – and today of all days.

Lauren came to the rescue, thankfully. "I'm not sure 'I'm sorry' is in Opal's vocabulary, but I think she does feel bad about it."

"What makes you think that?" Dee asked.

"Look how much time she spends needling you," Lauren said. "People don't tease each other like that out of genuine distaste. Either she thinks of you as a friend, or..."

"Or?"

"Or she has a crush on you."

"Oh, barf!" Dee said, miming putting her finger down her throat. "Never say that again!"

Rose started laughing – it was the first time Dee had heard her do that since Santa Cruz Island, and it was just as sweet a sound as it had been back then.

The zoo's resident herpetologist was waiting for them when they arrived at the tortoise enclosure, and his eyes lit up when he saw Rose. "Ms. Dennison, I've read all your research on giant tortoise mating in captivity, and I once saw you speak at Granville U. When Grace asked me for a favor I was happy to do it, but once I found out who it was for... I've been looking forward to this all week."

"That's so nice," Rose said, holding her hand out for him to shake. "What's your name?"

"Andre," he said. "Andre Smith."

"Well, Mr. Smith, I very much appreciate you doing

this for me," Rose said, and Dee recognized the admiration in the man's eyes. He didn't see a frail, sick old woman in a wheelchair any more than Dee did, and she hoped that Rose didn't feel that way in this moment either.

"Call me Andre, please. And it's just about feeding time," he said. "Want to give the tortoises their lunch?"

"I'd love nothing more," Rose grinned. "Lead the way."

They spent nearly two hours inside the tortoise enclosure, with three great old creatures that looked more like dinosaurs than anything that belonged in the modern world. Rose asked Lauren to wheel her right over to them, and she hand-fed them kale, dandelion greens and berries from the palm of her hand. Dee, Grace and Lauren all took turns too, but mostly they were just basking in the second-hand delight of watching a woman with so much joy written all over her face.

Rose was truly in her element, and she looked twenty-two years old again. At least in Dee's eyes.

They stayed as long as they could, and Andre was very generous with his time. At last, Rose was the one to suggest they ought to get back to Sunnyside. She looked at the gold-link watch on her slender wrist and said, "I imagine we've pushed our luck as far as we ought. Gina sometimes comes in the afternoons to help me get some fresh air – she likes to feel useful that way."

"She's a very dedicated daughter," Lauren said, and Dee admired her tact. She was more of a straight shooter herself, and probably would have called Gina possessive.

They said a reluctant goodbye to the three tortoises

and Andre, and Lauren drove them back to Sunnyside. Dee ditched her wheelchair at the front door and pushed Rose to her room, holding her hand while she eased down into her recliner.

"Would you like me to go now?" Dee asked reluctantly.

Rose didn't let go of her hand. Instead, she squeezed tighter. "You should stay a while. Would you like to?"

"Very much," Dee admitted.

Rose pointed to a mini fridge next to her dining table, offering Dee a sparkling water and asking for one herself. Dee popped a straw into Rose's and pulled a side table over the arm of Rose's chair, then sat down in the dining chair again.

"Did you have fun?" she asked.

"It was the perfect day," Rose said, her eyes going glossy with emotion. She looked away, busied herself with her water. Without looking at Dee, she said softly, "I do remember you, you know."

She looked at Dee and swallowed hard. Dee scooted a little closer. "I suspected."

"I could never forget you," Rose said. She held her hand out and Dee took it again. Their knees were touching now and Rose's skin felt papery and fragile, but at the same time soft and warm and familiar.

"I never forgot you either," Dee said. "Not for one day, or one minute."

"I'm sorry I pretended otherwise. I was... scared," Rose said. "Then, as well as now."

"It's okay," Dee hurried to reassure her. "You don't

have to explain yourself to me. I don't know how we got so lucky to end up here together, but I'm so glad you're here."

"Fate, maybe," Rose smiled.

"Or our subconsciouses leading us to make decisions that kept us in close proximity," Dee added.

"You're not mad that I ran away from you all those years ago?" Rose asked.

"Mad? Never."

"Regretful?"

Dee shook her head. "I'm eighty-two years old and I don't know how much time I have left, so I don't think it's a good use of my time to pine for what could have been. You lived a good life, right? You loved your husband, you have two children."

Rose nodded. "And you?"

"I've loved," Dee assured her. "I've traveled, I've enjoyed my career and I feel like I made a difference in the world. I've had a full life. I would not have objected in the slightest if you'd been by my side through all of it, but maybe we can make up for lost time now."

Rose squeezed Dee's hand. "I always admired you, you know that? Even back in the 60s, when we were so young, you knew exactly who you were and you demanded that everyone be okay with it. I was too caught up in making sure I was being taken seriously as a female scientist to worry about anything else."

"Did you ever come out?" Dee asked gently.

Rose shook her head. "I was married a year after I left the Galapagos, so there didn't seem to be much point. I followed all the civil rights protests in the news and I raised my children to be accepting and open-minded... but I never had the courage to come out myself. I bet you were right on the frontlines, though."

Dee smiled. "You think so?"

Rose returned the grin. "Just a guess. Even after all these years, I think I know you."

"You're right," Dee said. "After the Galapagos, I moved to San Francisco, lived there for about a decade, and in my free time I got pretty heavily involved in helping to distribute *The Ladder*. Went to a lot of protests and pride events in my day."

"Thank you," Rose said. "Even though I spent my life in the closet, I've no doubt your efforts have paved the way for an easier life for others." She went quiet for a moment, thinking and sipping her water. Then she said, "I know you said you don't need an explanation... but you should know something. About Gina."

"Okay," Dee said. "I'm listening."

"Excuse me," a sharp voice crackled through the air like lightning.

Dee turned to the door. *Speak of the devil,* she thought, looking at Gina standing in the doorway with her hands on her hips. Her eyes were on Dee and Rose's linked hands, and her expression was pure scowl.

"What are you doing in here?"

"Your mother and I are just visiting," Dee said, not letting go of Rose's hand.

"Well, my mother is sick," Gina said, coming into the room. "And she needs her rest. You need to go now."

"Rose can–" Dee was about to say that Rose was still perfectly capable of making her own decisions, but Gina grabbed the back of Dee's chair and she fully expected the woman to dump her out of it.

"Please," Gina said instead. "Let her rest."

Dee looked at Rose, and the meekness had leached back into her features.

"I'm sorry," Rose said. "She's right, I am feeling a bit fatigued. We'll finish our talk later?"

Dee let go of her hand, deflated. "Sure. I'll see you later, Rose."

She got up, not nearly fast enough for Gina, but a woman in her forties with two perfectly healthy hips was not going to rush her out of that room – for one, Dee didn't like her attitude. For another, it was a physical impossibility.

As soon as she was in the hall, though, the door clicked shut behind her.

Dee let out a breath, then started up the hall toward her room. Truth be told, she was pretty tired herself – mentally as well as physically. On her way, she bumped into Lauren and Angelique at the nurses' station. Lauren looked at her with anticipation.

"Well? Did you get what you were hoping for?"

Dee leaned on the counter to catch her breath and a smile slowly spread across her face. "I did. All in all, it was a great day – thank you."

15
LAUREN

"Are you sure all of your friends can be trusted with an ax?" Lauren asked as she and Grace pulled up to the bowling alley together that night. "And don't think I'm judging your friends – I'm just thinking of how clumsy my sister is."

Grace laughed. "I'm sure the facility will go over the safety rules. Nobody's going to lose an eye."

"Or a limb, I hope," Lauren added.

They parked, and Grace jogged around to Lauren's side of the truck. She stopped her in her tracks, pushing Lauren's back up against the passenger door to steal a kiss. Their bodies still pressed together, she asked, "Are you nervous about meeting my friends?"

"A little," Lauren admitted. "Who all will be here?"

"Marley, Blaire and Parker who you know," Grace said. "And then there's Parker's wife, Jules, Sonic's human, Syd, and her wife Adelaide. They have a son but he's too young for ax throwing."

"Anybody else?"

"Not tonight," Grace said. "I wouldn't want to overwhelm you with the whole crew at once."

"Which I appreciate," Lauren said. "I'm good with names – I have to be for my work – but usually I'm only meeting a couple people at a time at Sunnyside."

They headed for the building, and Grace asked, "Any word on how Operation: Tortoise Reunion turned out?"

"Yeah, Dee talked to me after," Lauren said. "She seemed a little bit disappointed – I think Rose's daughter cut the day shorter than she was hoping. But they both looked really happy at the zoo."

"They looked like a pair of long-time lovers," Grace said. "How crazy is it that they wound up in the same assisted living facility after all these years?"

Lauren smiled. "Makes you believe in soulmates or fate or *something,* doesn't it?"

"Something," Grace agreed. "I hope they're completely inseparable by the next time I come with the puppies."

"Dee's a very strong-willed woman," Lauren said. "I don't think she's going to back down."

"You're strong-willed too," Grace pointed out as she opened the door for Lauren. "You laid down the law with Gary and it worked out in your favor."

"For now, anyway," Lauren said. "But it did feel nice to speak my mind."

They found their group gathered near the entrance. Grace made introductions. Parker's wife Jules was rugged-looking, like someone who could swing an ax, and

Syd and Adelaide looked exactly like the type of people who would have a fennec fox – free-spirited and friendly.

Lauren glanced down at her own clothes, the same pair of slacks and blouse she'd worn to work but with flats instead of heels, and wondered what her own first impression said about her. Serious-minded, all work and no play, pragmatic? All of those things had been true before she met Grace. But now... she was a rule-breaker. A risk-taker.

A badass, if you asked Grace.

And, thankfully, all of Grace's friends were warm and welcomed her quickly into the group. A few minutes later, Lauren found herself sitting on a bar stool at the back of the ax throwing area, sipping on an iced tea and sharing fried mac n' cheese with Marley and Blaire. Grace stood beside Lauren, her arm slung casually around her waist, and the rest of the group were in the throwing area, getting instructions from the attendant.

The setup reminded Lauren of a gun range, but with handheld weapons. There were plywood targets at the other end of the room, and each throwing station was separated by long partitions of clear plexiglass. Everyone with an ax in their hand was required to wear eye protection, and no one was allowed to drink alcohol until they were done.

Still... watching Syd whip a fatally sharp object across the room and embed it in a piece of wood freaked Lauren out more than she expected it would.

Grace noticed the hesitance in Lauren's eyes. "You still feeling squeamish about this?"

"I guess I just spend too much of my day looking for dangers and risks," she said. "Can you imagine someone like Opal throwing an ax?"

Grace laughed. "I bet she'd love it."

"She would, but she's a maniac," Lauren cackled along with her.

They all took turns with the axes, and Lauren just kept deferring to the others in the group. She stuck to her safe zone at the bar table, sipping her iced tea and getting to know Grace's friends. They were all either vets or somehow worked with animals, and several of them owned their own businesses. They were a very impressive bunch, just as intimidating as the axes.

"Okay, everyone has thrown an ax but you," Grace finally said, taking Lauren's hand and pulling her to her feet whether she liked it or not. "Time to rip off the bandage."

"But–"

"It's fun," Grace promised, dragging Lauren up to the throwing area.

"It's fun watching you throw," Lauren said. Grace was in a tank top and jeans, much more appropriate ax-throwing attire, and her shoulder muscles bulged with every throw. Lauren couldn't tear her eyes away – and the view from behind wasn't bad either.

"I know you've got it in you," Grace encouraged, holding out an ax, handle first. "Just picture Gary standing in front of the target." Lauren gave her a horrified look, and Grace added, "Kidding! Good to know you're not even remotely violent, though."

Lauren accepted the ax, adjusting her grip. Grace retreated to a safe distance, and Lauren took a couple of practice swings, then let it fly. On her first throw, the broad side of the ax hit the plywood and it dropped to the floor. Grace handed her another one, and her second throw turned out much the same.

"Third time's the charm!" Blaire called from the bar table, and Grace gave Lauren another ax.

This time, it sailed through the air and embedded itself in the plywood with a satisfying *chunk!*

Lauren turned around with a grin on her face. "Okay... that was fun."

"Told you," Grace said. Behind her, all Grace's friends were rooting for her. Lauren had only known them for an hour, and they were all impressive as hell, and yet she felt instantly at home with them. They felt like family – just like Grace.

"Again," Lauren said, holding out her hand. Grace gave her a lusty smile as she slapped another ax handle into her palm.

"Go wild, baby."

16

ROSE

1964

After that first kiss, it was like a dam had broken in Rose. Everything she'd been keeping in, keeping suppressed, keeping hidden even from herself suddenly bubbled to the surface, and every last ounce of restraint crumbled away.

She thought about Dee every moment that she was awake, and she made regular appearances in Rose's dreams too. The woman even managed to steal Rose's attention away from the giant tortoises she came here for. She could think of little else but that kiss, the glimmer of want in her eyes, the promise of more on her lips.

'Next time' wound up being two days later. Rose was in the women's side of the latrines, a rather primitive building with a couple of shower stalls, a few toilets and a row of sinks – and far too many ants and mosquitos drawn to the moisture. She was alone, early in the morning before most of the research station had risen, standing at a sink with a towel wrapped around her chest and her toothbrush in her mouth. The door opened, and she stopped brushing when she heard Dee's low voice, gravelly with morning fatigue.

"Any more trouble with panthers?"

Rose spit out her toothpaste and wiped the corner of her mouth with the back of her hand. If Dee could be this confident and suave, Rose could at least attempt to match it – even if she felt nothing of the sort. She turned to face her, trying to be casual and natural in her bath towel. "I think you scared them off for me."

"Good," Dee said, coming closer. "You're up early."

"I like to have plenty of time with Frank and Margaret before the heat of the day makes them lethargic," she explained. "Plus, I only have a couple of months here... why waste time sleeping?"

"I agree. I hate wasting time."

Rose noticed a shower caddy in Dee's hand, and a towel slung over her shoulder, but she made no move to head to one of the stalls. All her attention was on Rose – something she wasn't used to. She quirked a smile at Dee. "So what are you doing standing here instead of taking your shower?"

"I'm trying to figure out if you'll let me kiss you again," Dee said, and her bluntness took Rose's breath away. She'd never known anyone this forward – a woman, no less.

You're already doing the impossible, she reminded herself. *What's one more thing?*

She stepped forward, leaving her toothbrush on the counter behind her. "I wish you would."

Dee set her shower caddy on the floor and scooped Rose into her arms without a second's hesitation. Their lips crashed together and Rose felt the knot of her bath robe pop open as she drew a long breath, inhaling Dee deep into her lungs.

This... this was just what she'd been waiting for, dreaming of, craving every moment since their first kiss. It was perfect, and it wasn't enough. *More, more, more,* Rose's mind and body begged in unison.

What is more? What comes next? She had no idea, but Dee seemed to sense her willingness, her desire, and deepened the kiss. Her tongue slicked along Rose's lower lip, then into her mouth. Her arms tightened around Rose's waist, their bodies a crush of longing.

"You're the most beautiful thing I've ever seen," Dee murmured between kisses.

"Thing?" Rose questioned.

"Woman... plant, animal, mineral... all-encompassing," she answered. "You're everything."

Rose went lightheaded – from the kiss or Dee's words or the way she was breathing, it was hard to say. "I've never been with a woman before," she confessed.

"You've never traveled halfway around the world on your own before either, I bet," Dee answered. Rose shook her head, barely breaking the kiss. Dee said, "I'm honored to be your first."

"First... what?" Rose's head was definitely swimming now, and she pulled back a bit, trying to catch her breath.

"Whatever you want me to be," Dee said. "I'm yours."

You're mine. I'm yours. Those words made Rose's heart race in her chest, they made her feel like running, but at the same time, she was exactly where she wanted to be.

Gravel crunched outside and Rose went rigid.

"Sounds like someone else is up," Dee said.

"You better go take your shower," Rose answered, still trying to maintain that casual air that was so clearly faked. She stepped away, hand going to her towel to reknot it. She turned back to the sink just in time for the door to open and one of the other women to walk in.

"Morning," she said.

"Morning," Dee answered – the picture of genuine calm and comfort in her own skin. Then she picked up her shower caddy and headed to one of the stalls. Rose stuffed her toothbrush back in her mouth before she was expected to make small talk.

---

*A*fter that early morning kiss, it was full-steam ahead. Rose never stopped feeling dizzy in Dee's presence, but she started to look forward to the feeling. It was intoxicating, being around her, and Rose's body thrummed with the desire for *more, more, more* whenever Dee was near.

They both got adept at stealing little moments together. Before dawn, after everyone was asleep, skipping meals to be together while everyone else was in the cafeteria. They ran off into the less-traveled paths in the jungle, and found quiet spots that belonged to just the two of them.

One day, they ate lunch atop a huge boulder overlooking a little stream and Dee told Rose about her research.

Another day, they stole away from their duties an hour early and hiked until they found a good spot to watch the sun set. That night as they walked back to camp, Rose told Dee about her life back home, and how Peter was just as much a thorn in her side at the university as he was here.

And one rainy day, when no one was working because it was just too dark and wet, Dee convinced Rose to throw on a poncho and follow her out into the storm. They ran as fast as they could to the small outbuilding where Dee had her workspace, and they were still drenched to the bone by the time they got inside.

Rose took off her poncho and laid it out near the door, then looked around the tiny space. There were three desks and a variety of scientific instruments that she assumed were weather-related, but which she could not have identified if asked. And Dee was pushing desks out of the middle of the room.

"What are you doing?" Rose asked.

"Making space. Want to give me a hand?" Dee had taken off her own poncho, and shrugged off the backpack she'd been wearing underneath. Both of their pants were soaked from the run, and water streaked down Dee's temples from her short hair.

"Sure," Rose said, taking one side of the desk.

They moved the furniture until there was a six-foot-square space in the middle of the single-room building, and then Dee opened her backpack. She pulled out the blanket from her bunk, along with a couple bottles of beer. "I figured we could have a little picnic here since no one's working today."

"A liquid lunch?" Rose teased as she helped Dee spread the blanket on the floor.

"There are candy bars and apples from the cafeteria in my bag too," Dee said. "Not the most elaborate picnic, but it was a last-minute idea inspired by the rain."

"I love it," Rose said.

She took a beer and sat down, and Dee immediately hooked her arm around Rose's waist and scooped her closer. "Come here. I want to feel you next to me."

It did feel nice, the heat from their bodies so intense that it was beginning to evaporate the raindrops on Rose's skin. She looked to the door. "Are you sure no one will come?"

"Well, truth be told, I hope someone's gonna come today," Dee said, and it took Rose a moment to figure out the meaning of her words, the innuendo. When she got it, her mouth dropped open and Dee grinned at her. "But no one's coming through that door, if that's what you're worried about. I locked it."

Then she kissed Rose, her hand sliding up Rose's ribs and over her shoulder, then along the column of her neck, gliding through the beaded raindrops. Rose tilted her head back, allowing Dee greater access, and was rewarded with Dee's mouth closing around her earlobe.

The sensation was exquisite and new, and it electrified her whole body.

She straightened her head again to look at Dee. She closed her hands around the collar of Dee's shirt, already breathing heavy with anticipation. And she asked, "How do we do this?"

"Are you sure you're ready?" Dee asked.

Rose nodded.

"I'll show you," Dee purred, then laid her down on the blanket.

Her hands traveled over every inch of Rose's body, slow and gentle, not grabby and impatient like some of the boys she'd fooled around with in the past. No, this was an entirely new and wonderful experience, and with the rain beating down on the tin roof above them, it felt like Rose and Dee were the only two people in the world.

Dee cupped Rose's breast in her palm, and warmth began to pool in between Rose's thighs. She squirmed beneath Dee's touch, her breath becoming faster and more ragged.

"Do you like this?" Dee asked.

Rose's eyes popped open, connecting with Dee's. She nodded eagerly, the words getting caught in her throat.

Dee smirked. "I thought so, just wanted to check."

Her hand dragged down over Rose's shirt and then back up beneath the fabric, skimming over her skin. "You're giving me goosebumps," Rose said.

"Oh yeah?" Dee asked, tilting her head to take a peek at the exposed flesh of Rose's stomach. "Yep, there they are." she bowed her head to kiss the bare skin and Rose sucked in a breath.

Dee was so close to her. This was more intimate than Rose had ever been with another human being, and certainly more than any other woman. Her warm breath against Rose's belly button made her whole body quiver, and she couldn't wait to see what came next.

Dee ran both hands up Rose's sides, beneath her shirt, lifting it to the level of her bra. "Is this okay?"

Rose nodded. "You don't have to keep asking me. I want to be here with you. I want to do this with you, only you."

"I don't want anyone but you either, darling," Dee said, then finished the job of pulling Rose's shirt up over her head. She tossed it aside, then swiftly pulled her own shirt up over her head in one smooth motion and threw it into the pile. When she lay down beside Rose again, the bare flesh of their upper bodies met and Rose wrapped her arm tentatively around Dee's waist.

"I'm scared," she confessed. "I've never done this before, with anyone. But I'm glad it's you."

"We can stop at any time," Dee warned her.

"I don't want to stop."

"Me neither," Dee said, hunger in her eyes as she took hold of Rose's hips and pivoted until they were both sitting up, Rose in her lap with her thighs wrapped around Dee. The warmth building between her legs built to a throbbing need and she found herself pressing her pelvis against Dee's firm lower belly.

"There she is," Dee said, clearly pleased with this

development. She took hold of both Rose's ass cheeks in her hands and pulled her even closer. The sensation sent a shiver up her spine and drew and involuntary gasp from her lips. "Go ahead, gorgeous, use me. Take what you need."

Rose's whole body thrummed and she wasn't sure she even knew how to do that, but Dee was looking at her with such unchecked desire, she wanted to try. She grinded her hips against Dee and lowered her mouth to kiss her.

it wasn't long before Dee had her naked and lying back down on the blanket. Dee was stripped nude too, and she took her time exploring Rose's body with her hands and her mouth. She slipped her fingers down Rose's stomach and into the wetness between her legs, and encouraged Rose to do the same.

"I'm sorry, I don't know what I'm doing," Rose said.

"If you would rather just lie back and enjoy, that's fine with me, darling," Dee said.

"No," Rose objected, her hand resting tentatively on the protrusion of Dee's hip bone. "I want to touch you. Pleasure you. I just don't know how."

"Do you ever touch yourself?" Dee asked.

Self-consciousness came rushing to the fore as embarrassment washed over Rose. She'd spent her whole life being taught that nice girls don't even talk about those things, let alone do them. But here Dee was asking with as much breeziness as if she'd asked Rose whether she'd seen the latest episode of *General Hospital*. Like it was no big deal, nothing shameful or secretive.

Maybe it wasn't.

"No," she admitted. She averted her eyes as she added, "I have used a pillow before, though."

"I think that's sexy," Dee said, turning Rose's chin to meet her gaze again. Not a single ounce of shyness in her eyes, how did she manage that?

"I'm afraid I'm not as worldly as you," Rose said. "Not as confident, either."

"That's okay, we'll get you there," Dee said, then winked. "In more ways than one."

She kissed Rose then, sinking her tongue between Rose's lips and drawing their bodies together on the blanket. She nudged Rose's legs apart and then wedged her own thigh between them, eliciting another gasp as she pressed herself firmly against Rose's center.

"For now, why don't you just use me like you do your pillow?" Dee instructed. "We have plenty of time to get to the other stuff later."

Again, embarrassment burned in Rose's cheeks, but not quite as hotly as what was going on between her legs. Spurred on by the hunger in Dee's eyes, she let her desires take control. She pressed her core against Dee's thigh, quivering already with the nearness of her release.

With the rain pounding above them and the rest of the research station none the wiser, the two of them rutted against each other, their motions becoming more frantic and their breaths turning to pants as they came together for the very first time.

And even though they only had a few months together, it would be far from their last.

17
GRACE

"What are you doing this weekend?" Grace asked as she watched Lauren in the bathroom mirror.

They were in the en suite off Lauren's bedroom, a spacious bathroom that was much nicer than the one in Grace's apartment. She'd spent the night, which was becoming a habit now that they'd finally broken through the intimacy barrier – now it was full-steam ahead, and Grace was loving it.

She was surprised by how much fun it was just watching Lauren get ready in the morning. Maybe it was something about the way she stuck her ass out while she leaned over the sink to get closer to the mirror. Or the way her soft cotton robe clung to her after she got out of the shower.

"No plans yet," Lauren said, meeting her gaze through the mirror. She was applying her mascara, far more of a perfectionist with it than Grace ever learned to be, but the effect was worth it. "Do you have something in mind?"

Grace's morning routine was much simpler. She'd already showered and slathered moisturizer on her face, along with a minimal touch of makeup, and now she was perched on the edge of the counter, simply enjoying the view.

"My dad had a cabin in the woods in southern Ohio," she said. "He always called it a hunting cabin but he was far too much of an animal lover to ever shoot anything. As far as I know, all he ever did was go down there with his buddies and drink. I haven't been there in years – since way before he passed. But I've been thinking about it lately. I guess it's mine now."

"You want to go?"

Grace nodded. "Probably should make sure the roof hasn't collapsed and the pipes didn't burst over the winter. We could make a little weekend getaway of it if you want to come."

Lauren turned around, bracing her hands backward on the sink edge. "You're inviting me for a romantic getaway? Our first?"

Grace hopped down from the counter and came to circle her arms around Lauren. "How romantic it is depends on whether any feral animals have broken in and made the place their toilet."

Lauren laughed. "Gosh, you know just what to say to a girl to rev her engine."

"I know, I'm irresistible," Grace said with a wink, pulling Lauren a little tighter. "So, wanna come?"

"I'd love to," Lauren said. "Although I guess it depends on how hectic things are at work this week. You know how they like to call me in on my days off."

"I don't want to criticize, but you need to learn to put your foot down a bit more – like you did with Gary," Grace said. "They need you, but not every waking minute."

"You're right," Lauren said. "I guess if we go out of town, they'll have no choice but to solve some problems on their own."

Grace nodded. "Put Angelique in charge – she seems to have a good head on her shoulders."

They kissed, and then Lauren pulled back. "Okay, we'll go to the cabin. But for now, you better let go of me. I need to be at work in half an hour."

"You're the boss," Grace said, retreating to her perch on the counter.

She was expected back at Granville Estates later this morning to see how everyone was getting along with Ham and Eggs, and she'd gotten a few more leads on potential partnerships with other medical facilities around the city that she needed to follow up on. It was only Tuesday, and they both had busy weeks ahead of them.

"All week I'm going to be dreaming of curling up with you in the big old hammock behind the cabin, looking up at the stars," she said. "I can hardly wait."

"That sounds wonderful," Lauren agreed. "We should bring a nice bottle of wine."

The cabin was on the edge of Mohican State Park in southern Ohio, a two-hour drive from Granville. Lauren and Grace went to the grocery store on Friday night after work to stock up on snacks and meals for the weekend, then headed out.

They spent the drive catching each other up on their weeks. Ham and Eggs were everyone's favorite residents over at Granville Estates. Rose seemed to be coming out of her shell thanks to Dee's influence – at least whenever Gina wasn't around to stop her. And by some miracle, Opal hadn't juggled a single breakfast pastry all week. She *had,* however, become obsessed with researching the cats at the local humane society, determined to find a way to adopt one.

"I think it's a great idea," Grace said as she drove. "I know Gary would have a coronary, but I'd be willing to bet Opal calms down and causes less trouble if she has a cat to direct her energy onto."

Lauren sighed. "I think it's a great idea too... Gary's like a huge immovable stone, though. He's looking the other way on the service dog visits, but I think that's the best I can hope for."

When Grace turned off the highway, the closest thing to mountains that Ohio had looming in the dark ahead of them, she put her hand on Lauren's thigh. "You work too hard, and you worry too much about your work. Make a deal with me?"

"What?"

"From this moment until we get in the car to drive home on Sunday, neither of us will talk about work," she said.

Lauren looked hesitant. "What if Angelique calls?"

"I'll make an exception for work calls," Grace said. "But if they get out of hand, I'm confiscating your phone. Barring a raccoon infestation in the cabin, I would love to spend the next forty-eight hours romancing and seducing you. You've never seen my A game."

Lauren grinned. "Whatever you've been doing so far has been pretty damn effective. Can I handle your A game?"

"Oh, you're gonna love it," Grace said, raising her hand to seal the deal. Lauren shook with her, and she said, "Now, let's hope I remember how to get to my dad's cabin – in the dark no less."

They got there, and the cabin seemed to be in excellent condition for one that had been abandoned for more than two years. No pipes had burst, the roof was intact, and there was no sign of so much as a mouse – a feat considering the cabin was nestled in a secluded spot deep in the woods.

They unloaded the food and other supplies from the car, and while Grace gassed up the generator and went around turning on lights, Lauren pulled dust covers off the furniture in the living room.

The space was small and cozy, a quintessential log cabin complete with a plaid couch and a wood-burning stove that did double duty as a place to cook and the cabin's heat source. Not that they'd need it in the middle of summer. Quite the opposite, actually.

"You okay with a mosquito or two?" Grace asked as she went to a window. "This place needs a good airing out."

"Fine by me," Lauren said. "It's beautiful in here. Well, except for the couch."

Grace laughed. "Hey, that's an authentic 1970s plaid pull-out."

"Exactly," Lauren answered while Grace went around opening a couple more windows.

The night air was cooler than the stuffy atmosphere inside the cabin, and the result was immediately relieving.

"What are you planning to do with it?" Lauren asked.

"The couch?"

"The cabin."

"I don't know," Grace said. "The practical side of me thinks I should sell it because I haven't been here in years and I'm too busy with my business to come down here often."

"And part of you wants to keep the place because it belonged to your dad?" Lauren guessed.

"Yeah," Grace admitted. "Come on, let's go hang the hammock while the inside of the cabin airs out."

She took Lauren by the hand and led her out the back door. There was a small patio with enough room for a dining table and a grill, and beyond that, just trees and hills and nature. And up above them, the stars.

Grace pointed to a pair of trees where the hammock

always used to hang. "I didn't have much time to come out here when my dad was alive either, but I do have fond memories of spending the whole night sleeping outdoors in a hammock between those trees."

She went over to a plastic storage trunk on the patio, pushed up against the exterior wall. Inside, she found what she was looking for – the hammock folded neatly, along with a handful of outdoor cushions for the dining furniture.

"Found it. Wanna help?"

"I have zero hammock-hanging experience, but I'll do what I can," Lauren said.

They figured it out, even in the dark. Then Grace went back inside the cabin to retrieve the bottle of wine they'd picked up at the grocery store. She met Lauren in the hammock, snuggling in next to her.

"We forgot to pack wine glasses," she said. "I could get us a couple of plastic cups from the kitchen, but I thought we might just drink straight from the bottle. Is that still romantic?"

"Who's around to tell us it's not?" Lauren asked, settling against Grace's side. "I like it out here. We make the rules."

"*Our* cabin in the woods," Grace mused. "I like the sound of that."

She took a sip and passed the bottle. Lauren took a sip, stealing a sideways glance at Grace.

"What?"

"Do you think it's time to have *that* conversation?"

she asked, passing the wine back. "Now that we're having romantic getaways and all?"

Grace smiled. "Which one?"

"The 'is there an us?' conversation. Is there?"

"Yes," Grace nodded. "Of course. As long as you'll have me, that is."

She could feel Lauren smiling beside her, even if she couldn't see it in the darkness. "So I'm your girlfriend?"

"And you're mine," Grace said. She set the wine bottle on the ground at their feet, then rocked them backward in the hammock so they could look up at the stars.

"They're so much brighter out here," Lauren said. "I love it."

"No light pollution," Grace answered. "Just the pure night sky."

"And you, and me," Lauren added. "Us."

"Us," Grace repeated. Then she kissed Lauren deeply, urgently, like there was no tomorrow and no world beyond the two of them.

18

LAUREN

The cabin was the perfect weekend getaway. By Saturday morning, Lauren could already picture making a point to unplug and come out here once a month or so with Grace, leaving their cell phones at the door and just coexisting for a couple of peaceful days. She could also picture a whole life with Grace unfolding before her – more than she'd ever been able to see with any other woman.

It was after ten and they still hadn't mustered the desire to crawl out of bed. They'd stayed in the hammock last night until the wine bottle was empty, then come inside and giggled their way through putting fresh sheets on the bed. Lauren had been warm and tipsy when she fell into it, her eyes already heavy with sleep as Grace scooped her into her arms.

This morning, they woke up to bright sun filtering through the window, and made love to each other slowly and attentively. Taking their time. Drawing out every last drop of pleasure from each other.

And they had the whole day to do more of the same, if they wished.

"I can't believe it took you so long to come out here," Lauren said, her head propped in the crook of Grace's arm. "It's heavenly."

"It would just be a sad, empty cabin if you weren't here," Grace said, kissing her temple. "You're what makes it heaven."

Grace's stomach growled and Lauren ran her fingertips over her bare, smooth skin. Grace drew in a breath.

"That tickles," she complained, and her stomach growled again.

"I guess we should get out of bed at some point, before we starve to death," Lauren said. Hunger had been gnawing at her own stomach for at least an hour, but she hadn't wanted to mention it, didn't want to end this moment.

"I've been thinking about the cinnamon rolls we packed," Grace admitted. "They'd go great with a cup of coffee."

"Should we go get them?"

Neither of them moved. Grace stroked her free hand over Lauren's breast, a possessive, gentle sort of touch that somehow managed to turn her on even more than a blatantly sexual squeeze.

"In a few minutes," Grace said, nudging Lauren's forehead until she turned her head to kiss her.

The kiss turned into something deeper, more urgent, their bodies turning toward each other, their legs entwining, their panting breaths becoming one. They made love again, more needful and desperate this time, and it was close to eleven before they finally dragged themselves out of bed.

"I can't remember the last time I stayed in bed that long," Lauren admitted, pulling on a T-shirt and a pair of pajama shorts.

"We'll have to come here again, then," Grace said. "Because I loved it."

"Me too," Lauren said.

They went into the kitchen, where they'd left all the food that they'd packed in a cooler. They didn't have much – they were only here for another twenty-four hours – but there was a refrigerator if they ever wanted to stay longer. Lauren found the cinnamon rolls and a bag of ground coffee, and Grace pointed her to the cabinet where the coffee maker lived.

While they waited for it to brew, Grace plated up a couple of oversized cinnamon rolls and they sat together at the small dining table beneath the kitchen window.

"What should we do with the rest of the day?" Lauren asked. "Feels like our little getaway is flying by."

"It is, too fast," Grace agreed. "Well, we could go hiking if you like. Or we could drive into Mohican and do the whole tourist thing – canoeing, zip lining, horseback riding. Or we could just chop some firewood and get the fire pit out back going, hang out here. You *do* have ax skills now."

Lauren laughed. "I'm not sure recreational ax throwing translates to chopping firewood."

"I think we should find out," Grace said with a wink.

The coffee pot stopped burbling and Lauren got up to fill their cups. When she came back, she set one down in front of each of them and said, "I'm sure you'd look much sexier chopping firewood than me. Especially if you do it in that skimpy tank top."

Grace was wearing a racer back tank that showed off her muscled shoulders, and with no bra underneath, her shoulders weren't the only thing Lauren was admiring.

"Skimpy?" Grace said, feigning offense.

"I can see your nipples from across the room," Lauren teased. "Strumpet."

Grace laughed. "Eat your cinnamon roll, prude." She arched her back just to emphasize her perky breasts, and she was lucky Lauren didn't lunge across the table and into her lap then and there.

The cinnamon roll was the tastiest, gooiest pastry she'd ever eaten – or maybe it was just the fact that they'd both skipped dinner last night in their eagerness to get to the cabin. And by some small miracle, they actually did manage to go for a long hike in the afternoon and get in a round of mini golf at the elaborate course at Mohican on Sunday morning. In between all of that, though, they couldn't keep their hands off each other.

"Thanks for inviting me out here," Lauren said when they were packing up the truck to drive home Sunday afternoon. "I really did need to disconnect for a while."

"Any time," Grace said. "I think I'll keep the place."

"Good. I might need a hideout when Gary finds out about the decision I've just made."

Grace arched an eyebrow. "And what decision is that?"

"I think Sunnyside needs a pet," she said, and Grace was already beaming.

"Seriously? I don't want to be the one who pressured you into it," she said. "Or put your job at risk."

"You didn't." Lauren chuckled. "Okay, you kind of did... but it's the right thing. Every week you bring the puppies and the residents light up. I swear I can see years melting off them – they sit taller and they smile more. And then the puppies have to go home and for the rest of the week, it feels like there's something missing, something leached out of the place. The joy is gone."

Grace had been about to hop into the driver's seat, but instead she jogged around the truck and threw her arms around Lauren. "You are the most incredible woman, and you have the biggest heart of anyone I know."

"Me? You're the one who literally can't stand still right now because you're excited on behalf of people who were strangers to you just a couple months ago," Lauren pointed out.

"They're my dad," Grace explained. "Every single one of them – I see him in all of them, and I know how much this is going to benefit them all. So, what are you thinking? Hamsters?"

Lauren shook her head. "I'm pretty sure Angelique would kill me if I asked her to clean out a hamster cage on top of all her other duties. And I think Opal is gonna get a cat one way or another, so if I beat her to it, I at least get to make sure it's not some street cat that's going to give everyone worms or something."

Grace laughed. "Domesticated cat, no worms, got it. What else?"

"I think it should be a shelter cat," Lauren said. "Somebody that needs a home as much as my residents need a furry companion."

"A lot of shelters put profiles of their animals on their websites," Grace pointed out. "I bet your residents would have fun looking through them to pick out the right cat."

Lauren laughed. "Opal definitely beat you to that idea – she's been scouting those pages for weeks now."

"Okay, it definitely sounds inevitable," Grace chuckled. "Come on, let's get on the road – I suddenly can't wait to get back to Granville." They both climbed into the truck, and as soon as they were on the road, Grace asked, "How are you gonna handle Gary?"

"Fuck 'im," Lauren said, and Grace's jaw dropped.

"Whoa, your badass transformation is complete."

"What?"

"I've just never heard you talk like that before," Grace said. "Maybe the fresh air was too much for you after all."

Lauren just shrugged. "You were right. I needed to disconnect for a few days and get my priorities straight. And my residents' happiness is my top priority."

"You're mine," Grace grinned, reaching across the center console to take Lauren's hand.

"You are *glowing*," Angelique said when Lauren got to Sunnyside on Monday morning. "Somebody got some good rest this weekend..." She lowered her voice to add, "Or good *something*."

Lauren winked before she could stop herself – the old her never would have done something so unprofessional, but the new version, the one Grace had awakened, couldn't see the harm in being friendly with her favorite employee.

She set her bag down and leaned against the nurses' station counter. "Grace and I had such a great weekend, and Mohican was beautiful. Thanks for holding down the fort."

"I am so glad she came in here with that cute little fox," Angelique said. "You've always been a great boss, but you were starting to look rough."

"Gee, thanks."

"You look happy and energized now, though," she added. "That's my point!"

"Well, how energetic are you feeling?" Lauren asked.

Angelique raised a suspicious brow. "Why do you ask?"

"I think we should get a cat," Lauren said. "I wanted to get your take first, though, because the idea is for the residents to care for it, but ultimately it'll be up to the staff to make sure it's being cleaned and fed, and that it's not getting twenty breakfasts a day from twenty different people."

"I love the idea," Angelique said without hesitation. "I'm in a tiny apartment with a no-pets policy, and I need a furry friend in my life."

"Great!" Lauren said. It was all coming together, and a relaxing weekend was all she'd needed to see everything clearly.

"What about Gary, though?" Angelique asked.

"Fuck 'im," Lauren said, and Angelique laughed and clapped her hands.

"Right on, girl! Err, boss."

"Don't worry," Lauren added. "If it blows up in my face, I'll claim full responsibility."

"I'm not worried about that," Angelique told her. "After I spent an hour talking at him about what I do here last time I visited, I don't think Gary wants to so much as look at me, let alone talk to me long enough to yell." Lauren gave her a questioning look and Angelique said, "After we talked charting, I treated him to a long explanation of sponge bath procedure."

Lauren laughed and gathered her things, shaking her head as she went to her office to start her day.

The residents were all on board when Lauren told them about her decision later that day – even the ones who would have rather had a dog. But dogs needed to be walked and trained and regularly exercised, and a cat fit much better with the needs of the Sunnyside residents.

The idea to let them choose their own cat turned out to be both a blessing and a curse. A lot of them became immediately invested in the decision, crowding around Opal's tablet every morning after breakfast to check the local shelters and humane society to see if any new arrivals had come in. By the end of the first week they'd found a six-month-old tabby, a three-year-old Siamese with icy blue eyes, and a hairless Sphynx cat that Opal was lobbying for.

"It looks like a Shar Pei," Cora said.

"Not the first place my mind went," Dee added.

"He looks like an angry ball sac, I know," Opal answered gleefully. "But that's his charm! Plus he's the most hypoallergenic option, what with having no fur, and it says on his profile that he was neglected in his previous home. He needs all the extra love he'll get from a big group like us!"

"I'm not sure I'd want to pet him," Cora complained. "Wouldn't it feel weird? Fleshy?"

"I thought you loved that," Opal teased, "what with all the romance books you read."

Cora made a face at her, and Opal swiped through the Sphynx's photos.

"There – he's wearing a sweater in that one. There are a lot of knitters around this place, do you really think we should deprive them of the opportunity to make little kitty outfits for the naked cat?"

Lauren kept waiting for everyone to come to a consensus on a particular cat. The tabby got adopted quickly – kittens always did – and the breakfast-time Kitty Selection Committee found a few more candidates.

There was a harlequin with gorgeous orange and

black fur. A black cat named Scissors that sparked lengthy debates as to what behavior could have given him that moniker. A long-haired Persian that was beautiful but who everyone agreed was probably too high maintenance.

And the Sphynx cat stayed on the humane society website day after day. Opal never stopped advocating for him, and one morning, Rose put her two cents in for the first time since the search began.

"My vote is for the Sphynx."

Dee turned to her. "Really?"

"He deserves a home," she said. "And Opal's right–"

"What's that?" Opal perked up.

"He's the best option for a lot of reasons," Rose went on. "Not least of which, he needs us."

The debate went on over several more breakfast meetings, until Rose and Opal had converted the whole group over to their way of thinking. And that was how Lauren found herself going to the humane society with Grace to pick up a hairless cat for Sunnyside.

19

DEE

On the day Lauren went to pick up the Sphynx cat from the humane society, a crowd gathered in the common room, waiting for his arrival. There was a raging debate going on about what his name would be, but Dee and Rose sat off to themselves in a couple of armchairs in the corner.

It had become their custom, ever since that day at the zoo – they'd lost sixty years that they could have spent together, and Dee was determined to make up for lost time.

Rose seemed to be on board, provided her daughter was nowhere around. Lucky for Dee, there seemed to be some sort of crisis going on at Gina's office, taking up more of her time than usual. Dee never forgot what Rose said at the end of the day after their zoo excursion – *you should know something about Gina* – but Rose hadn't brought it up again, so Dee didn't push the issue.

Anything that might drive a wedge between them wasn't something Dee wanted to address. Not now that she finally had her Rose back.

"What sorts of pets have you had?" she asked now. "You've spent your career with giant tortoises, so I can't believe you're a traditional dog or cat person."

Rose nodded. "You're right – I kept a pair of musk turtles in my office at the university. Ended up passing them down to the woman who inherited my office after I retired because they outlived my tenure. Might very well outlive me, in fact. But at home we had a mix of dogs and cats while Gina and Mike were growing up."

"I had a succession of Springer Spaniels," Dee told her, trying to ignore the quip about the turtles outliving Rose. "Great companions."

"But no human companion," Rose commented, reaching out to take Dee's hand. Her affection came naturally now, like they'd never been separated, but every time Dee noticed how pale Rose's skin was, how weak her grip had become, it squeezed at her chest.

"I had companions, girlfriends," Dee assured her. "Just none that went the distance."

Rose brightened. "You were waiting for me."

"Yes, I was."

"I'm sorry I took so long."

Dee squeezed her hand. "Will you..."

"What?"

This was something else Dee hadn't wanted to talk about. They'd spent every possible moment together over the past few weeks, talking about the past and enjoying the present. But the future... that was still a big, scary unknown. How much of it would there be?

Dee had to find out eventually. Sooner was better.

"Will you tell me about your prognosis?" she asked. "I know you're sick, but... how much time do we have together?"

The smile melted off Rose's face, and she squeezed Dee's hand. "Either one of us could get hit by a bus tomorrow – nothing is guaranteed."

"We rarely leave Sunnyside," Dee pointed out. "Not much chance of a rogue bus taking us out inside these walls."

"Okay, Opal could get her hands on a bullhorn and scare us so badly we have simultaneous heart attacks."

Dee grimaced, the pain in her hip flaring. She shifted into a more comfortable position, then persisted, "Seriously, darling. Tell me how much time I have with you."

The longer Rose delayed, the more panic filled Dee's chest. Was it worse than she thought?

Rose sighed. "I have stage three ovarian cancer. I had surgery, and tried radiation – several rounds, in fact – but it spread to my lymph nodes. I'm eighty-one. I decided I didn't want to spend the rest of my life feeling sick and tired. I moved here so that Gina and Mike wouldn't have to be the ones taking care of me, and I get all the pain meds I need to keep me comfortable."

Dee squeezed her hand harder, halfway worried she was hurting her with that grip. "So there's no chance..."

Rose laughed. "Of what? That I'll get better and live to be a hundred?"

"Opal's almost a hundred," Dee pointed out. "It's possible."

"I've lived a long and fulfilled life," Rose said, placing her other hand on top of Dee's. "My only regret is that you weren't in it longer."

"Me too. I never should have let you leave that island without me," Dee said.

"I wouldn't have let you," Rose said sympathetically. "The time wasn't right. But we have each other now. And now is all anyone really gets."

Dee managed a small smile. "Is it the cancer that makes you so wise?"

"The life experience, maybe," Rose said. "I should tell you about Gina now."

Dee's pulse quickened. "Okay."

"She knows about you–" Rose started to say, but then the common room doors burst open and the whole room exploded into chaos.

"They're back!" Opal cried. "Let me hold that bald, wrinkly baby!"

Grace held the door open for Lauren to come through with a cat carrier, then disappeared again. Lauren set the carrier on a table and said, "We got a whole pet store's worth of toys and treats, and Grace is going to build him a cat tree. She's bringing the stuff in from the truck now. Did you all decide on a name?"

"Nope, we're down to three choices, though," Opal said. "Mortimer, Anubis, and Yul Brynner."

"That last one seems like a mouthful," Lauren said.

"Well, open the carrier up and let's see if he looks like old Yul," Opal urged. "That'll be the deciding factor."

"Okay... give him room, though," Lauren cautioned. "He's nervous from the car ride and all the changes. We don't want to overwhelm him."

Dee stood and extended a hand to Rose, helping her out of her chair. They walked over to where the action was just in time to see Lauren moving the carrier to the floor. She opened the door and for a few seconds nothing happened. The cat crouched deep inside the carrier, unwilling to leave its security.

"Let's all sit down and be quiet," Lauren suggested. "He'll come out when he's ready."

"Opal, quiet?" Dee murmured to Rose. "Not likely."

They took seats with everyone else, and Grace came back a few minutes later with her arms full of shopping bags. She and a couple of the other residents unpacked them, setting a cat bed, a scratching post, and a couple of catnip-stuffed mice on the floor in front of the carrier.

"What were you going to say about Gina?" Dee whispered to Rose while they waited. She wasn't planning to push, but now that the subject had been broached...

"Maybe that's a conversation better had back in my room, or yours," Rose said. "Let's just see the kitty, then we can go."

"Okay," Dee agreed, though her interest had certainly been piqued now.

Mortimer-Anubis-Yul Brynner ended up being tempted by the 'nip. It took him about five minutes to get curious enough to come out of the carrier, tentatively pawing at one of the stuffed mice. The residents all talked in hushed voices to keep from scaring him back in.

"He's too pink to be Anubis," Cora pointed out. "And too feline. Anubis is a jackal."

"Just the right amount of pink for Yul Brynner, though," Opal pointed out. "And the perfect amount of bald too."

"You got to pick the cat," Dee pointed out. "I think you should let someone else have final say on the name."

"Should we vote?" Lauren suggested.

They made a show of hands, and Mortimer won by a landslide. Even the cat perked up his ears and paid attention at that name, so they all decided that his vote should be weighted accordingly.

"I can live with Mortimer," Opal agreed. "Plus, *mort* is French for death, and they say some cats can tell when someone's about to kick the bucket."

There was a collective groan, and Cora asked, "Could you not have told us that *before* we adopted him?"

"He's not going to sneak up behind you and trip you down the stairs, Cora," Opal answered. "Relax."

An hour later, Dee and Rose headed to Dee's room. They chose it for the privacy it allowed – even though Gina was busy with work lately and Mike's coping mechanism of choice had been avoidance ever since Rose got to Sunnyside, they didn't want to risk an interruption.

Dee, because she'd been waiting to hear this for weeks.

Rose, because what she had to say was obviously sensitive.

"Want some water? Cup of tea?" Dee asked.

"I'm okay," Rose said. "Think I need to take a nap after this, though. I get tired easily these days, and it's all the more frustrating now that I have someone I'd rather spend my time with."

"We could take a nap together," Dee suggested. Rose's cheeks colored, and she added, "Nobody around here is going to care. I made sure of that before I moved in."

"Gina will," Rose said. "If she finds out."

Dee finally stopped fussing with various things around her room and sat down next to Rose. "What did you want to tell me? You said she knows about me?"

Rose nodded. "She's not prejudiced. I need you to know that right off the bat. I would never allow my children to hold such close-minded ideas."

"Okay..."

"She's just upset about my cancer, and it's brought up feelings about her father's death," Rose continued. "She thinks that my spending time with you amounts to forgetting about her father, cheapening our marriage."

"How does she know about me, though?" Dee asked. "She slammed the door in my face the day you got here, before I said so much as a word."

"My photo album from the Galapagos," Rose explained. "She and Mike used to love looking through it, hearing me tell stories about the tortoises, imagining their mother on this grand adventure. And there were lots of photos of you in that book…"

20
ROSE
1964

The end of the summer came far too fast. Rose could have spent the rest of her life on that island, and by August, Dee was telling her that she loved her every single day.

Rose hadn't said it back. Mostly out of cowardice – for the fear of loving a woman, of giving her heart to anyone at all, let alone one she was imminently preparing to lose. It certainly wasn't because she didn't return the feeling.

Dee told her it was okay, she would say it when she was ready – or not at all, that was okay too. "I just need you to know how I feel," she said the day the ferry was scheduled to come and take Rose back to her old life. "I don't care if you don't feel the same, and I understand if you do but you can't say it. But know that I love you."

"I..." *Just say it,* Rose's heart demanded, but her head and her mouth refused.

They were sitting together in a small clearing in the

trees, on the same blanket they'd had their first picnic on top of on that rainy day back in June. The camp was behind them, the jungle stretching out ahead, and the time was ticking down audibly in Rose's ears. She was leaving today, any minute, in fact.

"It's okay," Dee said. "Just be with me, for as long as we can be."

Dee was staying on the island. Her own research wasn't concluded yet, and they'd joked that she'd probably get more work done in the two months she stayed on past Rose's departure than she'd accomplished the whole time Rose was here. And after that, Dee wanted to come find Rose, visit her in grad school, wait for her to get out and find a job. They could move together, start a life.

That was Dee's grand idea, anyway.

Part of Rose loved it, wanted nothing more. But the frightened, practical part of her said that she was already concerned no one would take her seriously as a female scientist. Add lesbian into that mix and how was she supposed to find work?

It was all she ever wanted. How could she give it up for a summer fling?

"I can't be with you openly," she'd said when Dee first broached the idea. "I wish I were as brave as you, but I'm just not."

"I understand," Dee said, although Rose could tell from the broken look on her face that she had hoped for more. A leap of faith Rose wasn't prepared to make.

"And I can't ask you to go back in the closet," Rose went on. "You are so vibrantly, beautifully *you*, I could never take that away for my own selfish reasons. It'd be like killing a part of you."

"You'll be taking a part of me with you when you leave no matter what," Dee said.

They talked about it again and again over the summer. Each time, Rose became frustrated and disappointed in her own fear, and she expected Dee to feel the same. But Dee only ever loved her harder, told her that she had to make the journey in her own time, in her own way.

And that she'd be waiting when Rose was ready.

Now, sitting on the blanket with Dee's arm around her shoulder, Rose felt the words *I love you* bubbling up in the back of her throat. But would it be cruel to say them when she'd been so clear about the fact that there was no future for them beyond the Galapagos? To drop those three little, enormously weighty words right before she left forever?

There was a rustling in the brush behind them and Dee took her arm off Rose's shoulder. She did it so casually, every time the secret of their relationship threatened to be exposed. Rose always jumped, guilt filling her belly, but Dee simply made a little extra space between them, unhurried and unbothered.

Peter stepped into the clearing. "There you are. Ferry's about an hour away. We need to go."

"Okay, I'll be right there."

He disappeared again, and Dee helped Rose to her feet. "I'm going to miss the hell out of you."

"I'll miss you too," Rose said, swallowing the lump

that was threatening to become tears. She didn't have the right to cry – she was the reason this goodbye would be forever. "I'm sorry... that I'm not braver. For you."

"If you ever change your mind, just send word," Dee said. "I'll be brave enough for both of us."

Then she kissed Rose, one final, slow caress to last her the rest of her life. And she let her go.

Rose went home. She spent her second year of grad school in a haze, trying to figure out who she was now and what she'd done by letting go of Dee. Some days, like the one at the end of the year when she landed a job interview at a highly competitive university, it felt like the right choice.

On other days, it seemed like the worst decision she'd ever made.

But it *was* made, completed, in the past, and so she slowly moved on with her life. Graduated. Let her mother set her up with Michael Moreno, who never made her heart flutter quite the way Dee did, but who was a sweet and intelligent man who loved her with all of his heart and who did everything he could to help her pursue her career goals. And in that respect, she achieved everything she'd wanted.

They got married. Had two children. Bought a house in the suburbs and got a puppy and lived a very nice and comfortable life. So what if their relationship never had the passion or the fire of that brief fling on Santa Cruz Island? You couldn't have it all, right?

Was it a mistake to leave Dee, to walk away from someone who made her heart sing like that? It was a question that kept Rose up at night sometimes. What would her life be now if she'd been less fearful, followed her heart instead of her head?

But by the time she had her first child, Michael Jr., there was no way she could label the path she'd chosen a mistake. And a few years later, Gina came along.

Still, the path not chosen nagged at Rose.

One cold fall day in 1982, when Gina was twelve and Mike was fourteen, the female half of the family got struck down by a vicious flu. Rose and Gina stayed home from work and school, cuddled up on the couch with bowls of chicken noodle soup and a humidifier blowing steam at them from the coffee table.

Gina had a whole box worth of used tissues scattered around her, and Rose had decided she didn't have the energy to keep nagging her to throw them in the trash bin, just a few feet away. Her head was pounding and her throat was scratchy, and she had her own runny nose to manage.

It was early afternoon and the TV had been on all day, *One Life to Live* making way for *General Hospital* in the soap opera lineup.

"No more TV," Gina groaned. "I'm so *booooored.*"

"You're sick, you're not supposed to be having fun," Rose reminded her.

"That doesn't mean I have to sit here and be tortured," she said, nudging the remote with her foot.

Rose rolled her eyes and reached for it. She turned off the TV, actually agreeing with her daughter's opinion on that one. "You want another ginger ale?"

"All of the fluid in my body has turned to ginger ale," Gina said. "No, Mom."

How did people deal with teenage girls, let alone sick ones? Rose closed her eyes, feeling the fatigue all the way in her eyelids. Her relationship with Gina wasn't bad, but the older she got, the harder it was to stay on stable ground with her. Mike was two years older, well into puberty, but he hadn't been nearly as volatile as Gina at this age.

When they both caught the flu, Rose had briefly thought it was actually a positive development – an opportunity for them to reconnect, be close the way they were when Gina was little and it was like having a mini-me following Rose everywhere. Baby Gina loved turtles and reading science books together and thought her mommy hung the moon.

Teenage Gina mostly hung out with her friends at the mall, and didn't hesitate to tell Rose how embarrassing she and Michael were whenever they dared show their faces outside the house.

But Rose and Gina had spent the last two days on the couch together, feeling like a Mac truck had managed a two-for-one special and run them both down. And none of the mother-daughter bonding Rose hoped for had happened. Mostly, they just slept and sneezed and stared with glazed expressions at the TV.

Then Gina coughed wetly and asked, "Hey, Mom?"

"Yeah?"

"When's the last time we got out the photo albums?"

Rose sat up a little taller. "You want to get them out?"

"Do you?"

There was the olive branch she'd been hoping for, and it didn't matter if Rose felt like death warmed over. She would muster every last ounce of her strength to go into the study and retrieve the family photo albums for her daughter.

She brought an entire armload of them out to the living room and set them on the coffee table. "We used to look at these all the time," she said as she picked up the first one. "It's been so long they're dusty."

"No, not that one," Gina said. "The turtles."

Rose smiled. She set aside Gina's baby book, the album she'd assumed her daughter would be most interested in, and picked up the well-worn album from her time in the Galapagos.

"Tortoises," she said. How many times had she looked through this book with Gina and Mike when they were younger, watching them *ooh* and *ahh* over Frank and Margaret, and yet Gina still called them turtles. By the smirk on Gina's face, Rose was sure it was intentional.

"Remember when I wanted to be a vet, or a researcher like you?" Gina said.

Rose tried not to sigh. She'd adored having a mini-me, and had been thrilled at the idea of her child following in her footsteps. Until last year, when Gina decided she'd rather be a fashion designer. "Yes, I still think you would have made a good one."

Gina shook her head. "I love animals, but that's way too much school."

"It's not so bad when you're doing it," Rose said. "It goes by fast."

"Show me turtles," Gina whined, sticking out her lower lip.

Rose opened the album, and Gina snuggled into her arm. They flipped through the book for twenty minutes, and Rose told Gina all the stories she always told about that trip. Peter had become the villain over the years, the two giant tortoises in Rose's charge were the scientists' pets, and the island itself had a personality.

And then there was Dee.

There were at least a dozen photos of her in the album, more than anyone else, barring Frank and Margaret. Sometimes just eating dinner with the rest of the crew, sometimes caught in the middle of a broad smile or a belly laugh that Rose could still hear simply from looking at the picture. And once, looking right at the camera, an earnest expression on her face.

Rose had considered taking that one out of the album, after the first time her kids asked to see the pictures and she recognized the pure expression of love in Dee's eyes. But she never did. She sometimes doubted her path, but she never regretted that Dee had once been on the same one. And she had no desire to erase her.

So she told the kids and Michael that Dee was her

best friend that summer, and that they'd gone on lots of adventures together. It wasn't a lie – it simply wasn't the whole truth.

"Did you ever talk to her again?" Gina asked now, when Rose got lost lingering over that intimate picture. "Mom?"

"Sorry, the cough syrup's getting to me. I think I dozed off," Rose lied. "No, we lost contact."

"Oh. Would you like to see her again?"

Rose looked at her daughter. "Of course. She was my best friend."

Gina nodded, and got quiet for a moment while Rose kept flipping pages, making comments here and there about the pictures as they came. Then, when they reached the end, Gina kept her eyes on the last page as she asked, "Were you in love with her?"

"What?" Rose's heartrate spiked.

"It's okay, I know about lesbians," Gina rolled her eyes. "A couple of girls in my grade are dating."

"Oh. Good for them."

"Well?"

"What makes you think that?" Rose asked.

Gina gave her mother a scalding look – the same *don't patronize me* look that Rose recognized whenever she said something unspeakably embarrassing in front of Gina's friends. "Come on, Mom. I'm old enough to notice these things. The way she's looking at you in that photo, the way you always linger on that page…"

Rose opened her mouth, and a fresh wave of shame washed over her. She couldn't say it now any more than she could eighteen years ago, when Dee was asking her not to leave. Why not? *Just say it!*

"I cared about her very much," Rose said, sinking lower into the couch, pulled by the gravity of her own disappointment.

"Do you love Dad?" Gina asked.

"What? Of course I do," Rose said. And that was true. She may not have had the same exact feelings him that she'd had for Dee on that island, but who was to say what true love felt like? Maybe the only thing she ever felt for Dee was lust. It was so long ago, and for such a brief time, it was impossible to say.

"So you're not a lesbian?" Gina persisted.

"Gina," Rose warned.

"*Mom*," Gina pushed right back. Rose studied her daughter's eyes, trying to figure this strange teenaged creature out, puzzle out what she was really asking. Ultimately, she didn't have to because for once in her life, Gina volunteered her feelings. "I don't care if you are, but... three different kids in my class have parents who are getting divorced. Are you gonna leave dad someday because you like women?"

"Oh, honey." Rose pulled Gina tighter against her, and for once, she didn't try to squirm away. "I'm not going anywhere, and neither is your father. We have a strong marriage, and that's not changing anytime soon."

She could feel her daughter relax against her. They kept talking for a while longer, and Gina opened up in ways she hadn't in months, if not years. She told Rose all about the various divorces happening around her, and her insecurities about love and relationships, considering how many kids she knew were beginning to date. And once the photo albums were forgotten, she even told Rose about Brandon, the cute boy in her math class who didn't seem to know Gina existed.

This was exactly what Rose had wanted out of their mutual sick days, and her chest swelled with motherly pride as she attempted to give her daughter all the right answers to guide her through the torment of her teenage years.

But in the back of her mind, she wondered. Why couldn't she admit how she felt about Dee, even now? And why couldn't she enthusiastically profess her love for Michael? A 'strong marriage' was important... but wasn't one built on a foundation of endless, passionate love even better?

21
LAUREN

The next week at work went surprisingly smoothly, considering there was a new four-legged resident running around.

Mortimer quickly adapted to his new surroundings, going from skittish to extremely curious and getting into anything and everything that he could. The cooks had to shoo him out of the kitchen more than once and then bribe him to stay on the other side of the door with a small bowl of wet food. Angelique said she once found him in the med closet – a feat considering it was locked at all times and closely monitored. And *Where's Morty?* quickly became a favorite game among the residents.

He took a liking to Opal in particular, which was good because she probably would have insisted on a second cat if he hadn't. And he already had a wardrobe of three different knit ensembles thanks to the enthusiastic knitters at Sunnyside.

"Have you told your Granville Estates people about Mortimer?" Lauren asked Grace one night over dinner.

"Yeah, and they're jealous," Grace snorted. "They think Ham and Eggs need another companion."

"Bacon?" Lauren suggested. "Teacup pigs are adorable."

So far, word hadn't spread to Gary, and the more Lauren saw the residents falling for Mortimer, the more confident she felt about her decision to bring him in. Gary would find out eventually – he was due for another site visit in a couple of weeks. But she'd deal with that when it happened.

In the meantime, Lauren was sure she'd made the right decision, and she tried to enjoy the little moments she caught sight of.

Opal bringing Mortimer down the hall to Cora's room for a visit and a little light smut reading. Rose looking so much more lively and happy ever since Dee suggested that trip to see the tortoises at the zoo. Anita styling Morty in his little outfits and taking pictures to send to her daughter, beaming the whole time.

One Wednesday afternoon, Lauren was sitting in her office working her way through an endless stream of emails when the newfound peace abruptly shattered.

Someone knocked hard on her doorframe, then stepped in before she could even look up.

"Ms. Carpenter," Gina Moreno hissed, coming to stand at the edge of Lauren's desk. "What kind of facility are you running here?"

She planted both hands on the edge of the desk,

towering over Lauren and staring daggers at her. Lauren rose to meet her at eye level and asked, "What's the matter, Ms. Moreno?"

"I did not bring my mother here so that she could be harassed by other residents," Gina snapped. "She's very sick and she needs to rest. That woman is in her room every single time I come here, no matter how many times I tell her to get lost!"

"That woman?" Lauren asked, though she knew perfectly well who Gina was referring to.

"Sandra What's-her-name," Gina said.

"Caldwell," Lauren supplied. "Though she goes by Dee. Would you like to have a seat and we can discuss this?"

"No, I want you to control your nosy residents!"

"I'm not... nosy," Dee panted from the doorway, chest heaving so much Lauren worried she might pass out. She must have practically run down the hall after Gina, a feat with that cane of hers, currently swinging from the crook of one elbow. "Rose and I are friends."

Lauren stepped around her desk and helped Dee to a chair. The last thing she needed was to refracture her hip. "Everyone sit down and we'll talk this out."

"I–" Gina started, but Lauren leveled her with an unbending stare.

"Please."

Gina huffed, but sat down beside Dee, arms folded over her chest. Lauren went to a mini fridge against one wall and pulled out a couple small bottles of water. She handed one to Dee, a silent request rather than a suggestion, and set the other one on the desk in front of Gina, who ignored it.

Lauren walked slowly back around her desk, hoping this would give Dee time to catch her breath and Gina time to control her temper. She sat, folding her hands on top of her desk. "Now. Ms. Moreno, your mother is entirely capable of making her own decisions about visitors, and she and Dee have formed a... friendship."

That was the word Dee had used, so it was the one Lauren would apply, though they both knew it was more.

"I know you would like to be here all the time for your mother, but that's just not practical," she went on. "You don't want her to sit alone all day, do you?"

Gina shot a scowl in Dee's direction. "It's not that my mother has friends. It's *her*."

"And what exactly is wrong with me?" Dee asked, sitting a little taller, looking ready to spit fire.

"You're insinuating yourself into my family," Gina said. "I warned you and you wouldn't listen."

"I have every right–" Dee started, but Gina whipped a stack of papers out of her purse and tossed them on the desk.

"Actually, you don't," she said. "I have power of attorney as of this morning, and I want my mother moved to a part of the facility where this woman cannot visit her."

Dee's jaw dropped. So did Lauren's, though her professional instinct kicked in quickly and she masked her expression. "Is this what Rose wants?"

"She wants me to oversee her care," Gina said. "We

always agreed I would get power of attorney when the time came. I just thought it would be when it was medically necessary, but if she can't be reasoned with then I'll do what's best for her however I can. Move her, Ms. Carpenter."

Lauren picked up the paperwork, unfolding it. She scanned it quickly – all pretty standard stuff, she'd seen a thousand powers of attorney before.

"Ms. Moreno, Sunnyside has a limited number of accommodations, and none of them are sequestered from the others," she pointed out. "Anyway, didn't you want your mother to have a view of the lake? The grass is mowed down now and it's really beautiful–"

"Fuck the lake," Gina snapped. "I don't care what you have to do, just keep *her* out of my mother's room or I'll sue."

Then she got up, thought for a second and snatched the unopened bottle of water, and stomped out of the office with it.

When she was gone, Lauren and Dee let out a collective breath, and Lauren saw the anguish in Dee's eyes.

"Can she do that?"

Lauren took another look at the paperwork, just to be sure everything was in order. "Unfortunately, yeah, she can. Has Rose told her family how she feels about you, as her friend or as..."

"No," Dee said. "She doesn't want to hurt them right before they lose her. Gina has it in her head that I'm trying to replace her father, and if Rose tells her the truth about our history... our present... I'm afraid it will only reinforce that notion."

"You don't think she would understand?" Lauren asked. "It is possible to love more than one person over a lifetime."

Dee gave her a sardonic look. "Have you met Gina?"

Lauren sighed. "Good point."

"So, what can I do?" Dee asked, gesturing to the power of attorney. "What can you do?"

"Legally? Nothing," Lauren said. "Gina has the right to make decisions about her mother's care, which extends to her living arrangements. She did say..."

She trailed off, wondering just how much risk she was willing to take on for this job. A cat was one thing – Gary could fire her for it at worst. But purposefully circumventing a power of attorney order, that could be a lawsuit, time in prison even.

"She said?" Dee prompted.

Lauren steeled herself. If risking her job to make her residents happy was worth it, then surely putting her freedom on the line was a fair trade for helping two people who were obviously deeply in love. *Soul mates?* she wondered.

And she couldn't help thinking about Grace. What would she do if someone tried to keep them apart? She would fight like hell.

"She said you weren't allowed in Rose's room," Lauren pointed out. "Please don't let Gina catch you talking to Rose until we get this sorted out because frankly, I'm afraid of that woman, as much as I hate to admit it. But your best shot is to talk to Rose while she's out of her room – at meals, maybe – and get *her* to talk Gina out of keeping you away."

Now it was Dee's turn to sigh, the weight of eight decades dragging her down. She hadn't looked this miserable since she found out Opal was her Secret Santa last Christmas.

"Hey, it's going to be okay," Lauren said, getting up and coming around the desk. She sat in the chair beside Dee and put a hand on her shoulder. "You two found each other after how many years apart?"

"Sixty."

"Sixty years, and you wound up here together. That's a *miracle,*" Lauren said. "And I know you're one hell of a fighter. You were working your way up and down the hallways just days after your hip surgery."

"They said it was the best chance I had for a full recovery," Dee offered.

"And you did it because you knew it would help, even though I bet it hurt like hell."

"You can say that again," she snorted.

"I have to obey this power of attorney order because I work here, but you don't," Lauren said. "You can work around it and I know you won't give up on your girl. You haven't in all this time."

Dee gave her a feeble smile. "Thanks for the pep talk."

"Anytime," Lauren said, then added, "just don't be the reason I get sent to jail."

"I'll visit you," Dee said, and they both laughed. Dee

started to get up, and Lauren helped her to her feet. "You and Grace, that going good?"

Lauren blushed. She'd been trying to keep that quiet, but Angelique and a few other staff members had picked up on it. In a microcosm like Sunnyside, it was only a matter of time before the residents did too. "Yeah, I think I love her."

"Well, don't waste any time," Dee said. "It's precious, and you never know how much of it you've got."

22
GRACE

Grace was at Sunnyside a few days later for puppy play time, and even if Lauren hadn't briefed her about what happened between Dee and Gina, she would have been able to feel the difference in the air.

Dee was present, playing with her usual poodle mix, but without any of her typical enthusiasm, and without her partner by her side. Rose was nowhere to be seen, and after a few minutes in which Dee kept glancing toward the door, obviously hoping Rose would make an appearance, Grace whispered to Lauren, "Is Gina here today?"

"Of course," Lauren said, barely suppressing a grimace.

"So, no chance Rose will make it to puppy play time."

Lauren just shook her head. "I'm sure Gina will be here even more than usual until she's sure that I'm enforcing her request to keep Rose away from Dee."

"Ugh, how can anyone be so awful to their own mother?" Grace wondered.

"I don't know, babe," Lauren shook her head. "She thinks she's doing the right thing."

Grace opened her mouth to answer, but recoiled as an ear-splitting yelp broke the peace of the room, followed by utter chaos. "What on earth?"

She and Lauren both jumped into the fray, figuring out the problem as they went. Grace lunged for the puppy that had cried out, the pure white Great Pyrenees that Rose usually played with named Snow. He now had blood pouring down one ear and was crying loudly. Lauren corralled her residents backward, out of the way, and Grace saw Opal crouching down and calling out to Mortimer, who was under a chair hissing like mad.

"Who let him in here?" Lauren asked. "We agreed, no cat in the common room while the puppies are here!"

"It's okay, Mort, relax," Opal said, yanking her hand back as he swiped at her.

"Opal, step back please," Lauren said. "I'll get him."

The puppy was still howling in Grace's arms, and she had one hand clamped over his ear to apply pressure. Well-meaning residents were crowding around her, trying to comfort him and help but only succeeding in making Grace feel claustrophobic. She bounced the puppy like a baby. "It's okay, sweetie, you'll be okay."

One of the caregivers, Miguel, appeared with a stack of napkins from the kitchen to help staunch the blood flow.

"Is he okay?" Lauren asked, her attention torn

between the hissing cat, her frantic residents, and the yowling puppy.

"I think he's mostly scared," Grace said. "I should take him to Marley, though, in case he needs stitches."

"I can go with you," Lauren offered, although she was also attempting to scoop an angry, sweater-wearing cat out from under a chair at the same time.

"You stay here," Grace said. "I'll handle it, and call with an update."

"Okay, well, you can borrow Miguel if he doesn't mind," Lauren said, and he nodded.

"Yeah, I don't mind," he said. "Do you want me to drive so you can keep pressure on the wound?"

"That'd be great," Grace said. She spared one more sympathetic look in Lauren's direction – she really didn't want to leave her to deal with this mess by herself – but the puppy's ear was making a mess down the front of her shirt, and that had to take priority. "Okay, Miguel, let's go."

They took Grace's truck, and Miguel proved to be a level-headed ambulance driver. He got them to Marley's clinic in fifteen minutes. Grace called ahead while they were driving, and Marley met them in reception as soon as they arrived.

"Let me see," she said, gently peeling back the napkins from the puppy's ear.

He'd stopped crying on the ride over, but he was still quivering in Grace's arms. "Got attacked by a cat," she explained again, even though she'd already told Marley as much on the phone. "How's it look?"

"Not too bad," Marley answered. "He might need a couple of stitches, but I'm confident he'll live. Come on back."

"Umm, stitches?" Miguel asked. "I don't really do any of the medical stuff at work. I don't know if I want to…"

Marley pointed to a row of chairs across from the reception desk. "You can wait out here. It shouldn't be too long."

"Thanks," he said, gratefully retreating to a chair.

Marley led the way to an exam room, then told Grace to set the puppy down on the table. She took one look at the front of Grace's shirt and laughed. "Thank God you didn't also want to wait out there. I don't want people seeing *that* first thing when they walk in the door. They'll think we murder animals instead of healing them."

Grace looked down at herself. She'd been able to feel the wetness spreading, but she really did look like she'd just finished committing a violent crime. "Well, this shirt is toast. How's my guy?"

"Ears bleed like hell," Marley said, already examining the pup. "But it looks a lot worse than it is. Appears to be clotting well so we might not need stitches after all." She raised her voice to call into the hallway, "Hey, Ling? You available?"

"Yes," someone called, then a young woman in cat-print scrubs appeared. "What can I do for you, boss?"

"I need some antiseptic and gauze to start," she said, and Ling disappeared once again.

"Is Erin going to kill me?" Grace asked. "I let her dog get hurt."

"These things happen," Marley said. "We'll get him patched up and back to his gorgeous, fluffy self."

"Thanks, Mar." Grace took a breath, realizing that her heart had been in her throat this whole time. "Do you mind if I step out to call Lauren, let her know he's okay?"

"Sure. Uh, can you use my office instead of reception though?"

Grace laughed, looking down at her shirt again. "Yeah, no problem."

She passed Ling in the hall, her hands full of first aid supplies. Grace checked in with Miguel, who was playing with his phone, then went to Marley's office and took out her phone.

It rang a handful of times before Lauren picked up. "Babe? Is he okay?"

"Yeah, the bleeding stopped and Marley said he probably doesn't even need stitches," Grace hurried to reassure her. "You get everything under control on your end?"

Lauren sighed. "Well, puppy playtime came to an abrupt end because all the other dogs were freaked out by what happened to Snow, and I called Erin to come take them back early. She and the nurses wrangled them into their crates, and she said she'll be headed your way to pick up Snow as soon as she gets the rest of them home and settled."

"Great," Grace said, pinching the bridge of her nose. "I'll call her after we finish, let her know not to worry. What about Morty?"

"Currently curled on my lap, purring like he's never

done anything wrong in his life," Lauren said. "And you'll never guess who decided it was a good idea to bring him to puppy playtime."

"Opal," they both said at once.

"I swear, some days I want to tie that woman to her bed," Lauren said, and Grace couldn't help laughing at the visual. It was the wrong thing to do, apparently, because Lauren snapped, "This isn't funny! Snow got hurt and Erin's pissed off, and Cora nearly passed out at the sight of all that blood!"

"I'm sorry," Grace said. "You're right, but it'll all be okay. Snow's fine, and I'll smooth things over with Erin–"

"I don't know what I was thinking," Lauren said. "You got bit by one of those hamsters on their first day at Granville Estates. That should have clued me in that this was inevitable."

"Lauren–"

"This is the whole reason Gary is so dead-set against the animal idea, because of the legal liability," Lauren went on. "What if Morty attacked a resident instead of Snow? Have I been foolish and naïve about this whole thing?"

"He didn't attack," Grace argued. "He just got scared and did what animals do."

"Yeah, that's the problem," Lauren said. "I have enough unpredictable people around here. Maybe it wasn't such a good idea to add a strange animal into the mix."

"Can we talk about this when I get back?" Grace asked.

She heard Lauren sigh over the phone, and wished she was there to put her arms around her, to help her put all this into perspective. Lauren was panicking, and Grace hated not being there to help fix the problem she'd created.

"Yeah, I guess. I gotta go."

"Okay–" Grace said, but Lauren had hung up.

There was a pit in her stomach when she got back to the exam room. Marley was just finishing up a bandage on Snow's ear, and Ling was holding him still.

"What you have right here is a very good boy," Marley said. "He's going to heal up just fine." She noticed the stricken look on Grace's face. "Everything okay?"

"I think I screwed up with Lauren."

"Uh-oh. Ling, can you go keep an eye out for Erin from the service dog training school?"

Ling nodded, and headed out of the room. Marley set Snow on the floor and he immediately started sniffing every corner, following every intriguing scent. Marley closed the door so he couldn't go far – or maybe so she could talk to Grace.

"She's upset about the puppy?" she guessed. "It's really not a big deal – the cut will heal in no time, and Erin's an understanding person. She knows puppies get into things – including cats' faces, apparently."

"She's worried she made the wrong call," Grace said, "and I have to admit, I'm worried I pushed her into all this. I wanted Sunnyside for my business, and then I wanted it because it was an excuse to get close to her. I never *really* stopped to think about the consequences for her."

"Keeping all this from the boss, you mean?"

Grace nodded. "Maybe we moved too fast."

"Are we talking about your business or your relationship?" Marley asked.

"Both?" Grace crouched down to pet Snow and inspect his newly bandaged ear. "What do you think, Mar?"

"When Blaire and I first started dating, I was the one who moved way too fast," she answered. "I couldn't help it – I'd basically given up on love, and then here comes my soul mate, just waltzing into the clinic with an elderly Shiba Inu. I knew it was love at first sight, but it took Blaire a while to see it too. You know what I didn't do?"

"Smother her with bunnies and puppies and Sphynx cats?"

Marley laughed. "No, I did not do that. But I also didn't give up. I gave Blaire the time she needed to heal her broken heart and when she was ready, I was there for her."

"So you're telling me to give Lauren time," Grace said.

"I'm telling you that you have to hold onto a good thing when you find it," Marley said. "And maybe you're both right – maybe you balance each other out. For as long as I've known you, Grace, you've always thrown yourself headfirst into anything and everything that interests you. Sometimes that's a wonderful thing, and sometimes a little bit of caution would have been better. Maybe Lauren is the caution to your recklessness."

There was a soft knock on the door, then Ling poked her head in. "Erin's here."

"Send her back, thanks," Marley said. When she was gone, Marley turned back to Grace. "You good?"

"Yeah, thanks."

Erin appeared a moment later, her eyes widening when she saw the blood on Grace's shirt. She got right down on her knees and scooped Snow into her arms. "Oh, what did that mean cat do to you, baby?"

Snow was all smiles and wagging tail, all memory of the traumatic event seemingly forgotten. Grace, on the other hand, could still hear his pitiful cries.

"Erin, I am so sorry," she said. "It was an accident, but I should have been quicker–"

"It's okay," Erin interrupted. "Lauren explained what happened, that Morty was never supposed to be in the room and they both just got scared."

"Well, I'll take care of the vet bill," Grace said, and Erin laughed.

"I won't fight you on that. But don't worry, I'm just glad Snow is okay."

She took Snow and left, and Grace and Marley made small talk for a little while. Marley suggested bowling that weekend, and Grace said, "Hopefully Lauren will be up for it. She really liked all of you when we went ax throwing."

"We liked her too," Marley said. "And I like her for

you. You two suit each other. Oh, and don't worry about Snow's bill – it's on the house."

"No, I insist," Grace said. "Just because we're friends doesn't mean – oh shit."

"What?"

Grace laughed. "I left that poor Sunnyside guy out in the lobby forever ago. Kinda forgot about him."

"You better go," Marley said, then added, "Wait just one more second." She disappeared down the hall and came back a minute later with a scrub top in her hand. "He seems squeamish, and I don't think you should go out in public looking like that."

Grace took the scrub top. "Good call. I wouldn't want to give Miguel a medical emergency too."

Marley went up front, and Grace peeled off her ruined shirt and threw it in a bio-waste bag before pulling on the scrub top. She went out to the reception area and settled the bill, then went over to Miguel. "Okay, field trip's over. Let's get you back to work."

23
LAUREN

Today seemed tailor-made to test Lauren's competence as an administrator, and at the moment, she didn't feel like she was passing that test.

She'd basically been right in the middle of a sentence on the phone with Grace when Gina burst into her office, and her first thought was, *oh crap, what now?* But the look on Gina's face wasn't her usual vitriol – it was fear.

"I gotta go," Lauren said to Grace and hung up the phone. "Gina, what's wrong?"

"My mom just collapsed in the hallway!" she said, tears streaming down her face.

"What?" Panic shot through Lauren's sternum. She was on her feet in a second, dumping poor Mortimer on the floor. He seemed to understand, dodging out of her way as she barreled out of her office, shouting, "Code blue, I need a nurse over here!"

"We were taking a walk," Gina mumbled, pacing behind her. "And she just *dropped.*"

Angelique was the first on the scene, and Lauren was relieved to let her take over. Everyone in the building was trained in CPR and first aid, but Lauren felt much more comfortable being the one to call for an ambulance. Angelique was on her knees, checking Rose's vital signs and calling her name, calm and in control the whole time.

"911, what is your emergency?" the operator said in Lauren's ear.

She'd dialed purely on instinct, and now she had to pause to ask Angelique, "Is she conscious?"

"No," the nurse answered. "But I've got a pulse. Her breathing is labored."

Lauren relayed everything to the 911 operator, and Gina kept pacing beside her. It didn't take long for the other residents to notice the new commotion, and Dee pushed her way to the front of the gathering crowd.

"What happened?"

"She collapsed," Lauren told her.

Gina mustered a bit of her old, nasty self to hiss, "Don't talk to her about my mother's condition!"

"I'm sorry, Gina, but anyone with eyes can see that she collapsed," Lauren said before she could bite back the words. The woman looked like she'd just been slapped, and Lauren sucked in a breath. Gina's mother was having a medical emergency, and here was Rose's caregiver, yelling at her. "I'm sorry."

"You should be." At least it stopped her pacing. Now she was standing with her hands on her hips, fire in her eyes.

"Angelique has got this under control, and the ambulance is on its way," Lauren assured her. "Maybe you'd like to use my office to call your brother, so he can meet you at the hospital?"

"I'm not going anywhere," Gina said, but after a moment's consideration, she pulled out her phone and dialed a number. "Mike? Something happened to Mom."

Lauren stole a glance at Dee, who was wringing her hands in the universal gesture of helplessness, watching Angelique's attempts to revive Rose.

The wail of a siren swelled in the distance, and soon Lauren could see the flashing red and white lights through the hallway windows. "I'll go out and meet them," she told Angelique, who was checking Rose's pupils for dilation.

"She's coming around," Angelique said, so at least that sounded hopeful.

Lauren jogged out to the parking lot, damn near twisting her ankle in her heels. Why the hell was she still wearing those stupid things to work, when every day was a new and unique disaster?

Because professionals wore suits and heels to work. Because she wanted to be taken seriously. Because she wanted to be the best damn facilities director she could be.

Who disobeyed her direct supervisor on multiple occasions, and mixed her personal feelings with work programming, and found loopholes in legal requests made by her residents' families. Yeah, she was doing a real bang-up job lately.

In the parking lot, Lauren met Grace and Miguel

coming back from the vet clinic at the same time that the ambulance pulled up.

"What the hell's going on?" Grace asked. "This isn't all because of Morty, is it?"

"No," Lauren said. "Rose collapsed."

"How can I help?" Miguel asked.

"Show the medics where to go," she told him. "She's in the hallway outside my office."

He nodded, then ran over to meet the paramedics as they pulled a stretcher out of the back of the ambulance. Ran in his sensible sneakers, Lauren noted.

She should go back inside with them, but she also really needed a second or two to breathe. "How's Snow?" she asked.

"He's fine," Grace reassured her. "No stitches, even, just a bandage. Erin came and got him."

"Good," Lauren said. "Do you think that's the end of puppy playtime?"

Grace shook her head. "Erin was worried, but not mad. It'll be fine. I'm sorry I pushed you so hard about the animals. I guess you were right after all – I wasn't thinking about all the possibilities, all the liabilities."

"I have to get back in there," Lauren said. "We can talk about that later, okay?"

"Okay." Grace grabbed Lauren's hand before she could turn to walk away. "Hey."

"Hmm?"

"I... care about you. A lot," Grace said. It seemed like a different word had been on the tip of her tongue, one that started with L.

Lauren smiled. "I care about you too."

"Call me once things settle down?"

"Yeah."

"I hope Rose is okay."

"Me too."

Lauren headed back inside, and Grace turned toward her truck.

In the hallway, Rose was being lifted onto the stretcher and her eyes were open now. She had an oxygen mask over her face, and Lauren smiled when she noticed that she was holding Gina's hand on one side, and Dee's on the other. Gina was either so distracted she didn't notice, or her bandwidth for caring had been exceeded for the moment.

"Are you both family?" one of the medics asked them.

Dee threw a pleading look to Gina, whose eyes went to her mother's hand clasped in Dee's. Lauren knew she should just stay out of it – especially knowing that Gina had already gone so far as to get power of attorney just to keep them apart. But a good facility director advocated for her residents, and everyone could see what Rose's choice was.

Lauren stepped up and gently placed a hand on Gina's shoulder. "Your mother will want her there at the hospital – she wants both of you."

Gina let out a breath through gritted teeth, as if it were painful to say the words. But she said them. "Yes. She can come."

"Miguel, can you get a wheelchair for Dee?" Lauren

said. "Or if it would be better, I can drive her to the hospital."

"Yeah, actually, we only have room for one ride-along," the medic said apologetically.

Gina rolled her eyes. "Oh, for God's sake, just let her go with you. I have to pick Mike up from work anyway, his stupid car broke down today of all days!"

"Thank you," Dee said, but Gina wouldn't meet her eyes.

The paramedics got on the move, Miguel, Dee and Gina following them, and the rest of the residents and staff started to clear out of the hallway now that the excitement was over. Lauren took another deep breath and glanced at her watch – all of this and it was still only three p.m. She had a couple hours left on her shift, and hadn't had time to do any of her usual duties.

And she wasn't going to get to them any time soon, because as the crowd thinned, she noticed Gary standing in the hallway, his customary clipboard in hand, a stern expression on his face.

Oh shit. What's he doing here?

She plastered on a smile – fake as hell and obvious from a mile away, but it was the best she could do. "Mr. Peterson, hello! What brings you to Granville? I wasn't expecting you for another month."

He narrowed his eyes at her. "I thought I'd bump up my quarterly visit just to make sure everything's running smoothly here."

Just to make sure I'm not doing anything I promised I

wouldn't, Lauren surmised, and if that was the case, Gary had plenty of reason to be suspicious.

"Although from the looks of it, I'm not so sure that's the case," he added.

"We had a medical emergency this afternoon," she explained. "One of our residents collapsed, which is unfortunate but with an elderly, sick population–"

"I wasn't talking about that," Gary said. "I heard something about an injury during your little doggy daycare program?"

Sonofabitch! Lauren cursed internally. That happened a couple of hours ago – who the hell was snitching to Gary, and why?

"Yes, there was an incident," she said, trying to keep her calm. "But none of the residents were injured and the dog will be just fine. And it's a puppy playtime to help socialize future service dogs, not doggy daycare."

"And how did this injury occur?" Gary asked.

How much did he know? Did the snitch tell him about Mortimer? Lauren decided not to show her hand until she absolutely had to. "Oh, you know, puppies are energetic and accidents happen…"

Gary nodded to the open door behind her. "Let's go into your office and talk."

Shit. "Uh, okay. Can I get you a coffee, water–"

"Now."

Well, this wasn't good. Lauren stepped aside, holding her arm out to welcome him in. Gary took a step forward, and just as he crossed the threshold, Mortimer zoomed out from under Lauren's desk and across Gary's feet.

"What in God's name– That is the biggest rat I've ever seen in my life!" he shouted, practically climbing the doorframe to get away from Morty. Lauren would have laughed if she wasn't in it up to her eyeballs.

"That," she sighed, "is Mortimer. He's a Sphynx cat, not a rat."

"And what the fuck is he doing here?"

Getting me fired, Lauren thought.

That was exactly what happened in her office. Gary got angrier and redder than she'd ever thought him capable – up til now, he seemed only capable of getting emotional about spreadsheets and the budget. And Lauren just let him vent, because she deserved every criticism he passed down.

She had gone behind his back, numerous times, and if the tables were turned and she was in his shoes, she'd be just as frustrated as he was.

She didn't blame him for firing her – she only wondered what the hell had gotten into her to make her so disobedient.

Grace. That's what – or whom.

Lauren packed up her office, all her personal effects fitting into a single, stereotypical cardboard banker's box. Where did those boxes even come from, anyway? Did companies just keep stores of them for when they needed to fire people?

"And take the cat-rat-thing with you," Gary said. "It can't stay here."

"Please, no," Lauren said. "The residents will be crushed—"

"Absolutely not," Gary answered, hands folded tightly across his chest.

Lauren nodded, hanging her head. "Okay. Just let me put my stuff in my car and I'll come back to get him—"

"One of the staff can help you transport him," he said.

Right, because if she was allowed back in the building once she'd been escorted out, Lauren might make a scene. Steal supplies. Rile up the residents. Heaven forbid. "I'll ask Angelique," she said.

Gary followed her out of the office and down the hall to the nurses' station. Lauren felt like a criminal of the worst kind, being marched to her death. A few residents came to watch the debacle, and Opal asked, "What's going on, boss?"

"I'm not boss anymore," Lauren explained. "I'm so sorry, I have to take Morty with me."

"*What?*"

Gary kept her marching forward, and it was probably the only favor he'd ever done her. She didn't actually want to stand there explaining to Opal how she'd gotten her hopes up about the cat only to rip him away. She'd find out all the details soon enough.

"Angelique?" Lauren called when they got to the nurses' station and found it empty.

Angelique wasn't around, but one of the other nurses

came over. "Ms. Carpenter?" She caught sight of the banker's box. "What's happening?"

"I'm... leaving. And I could use a hand," she said. "Will you help me track down Morty?"

Between the two of them, they found him curled up on Cora's bed and wrangled him into his carrier. Lifting him off Cora's lap was even worse than telling Opal he was leaving, and Lauren felt awful taking him away without so much as letting the others say goodbye. Gary strictly forbid it, wanting her and her cat out of the building as swiftly as possible.

Twenty minutes later, she sat on the floor in her spare bedroom, the carrier open beside her, Mortimer zooming around the room and checking out his new surroundings. She knew she needed to go out again, get him food and water bowls, a litter box, toys – all the stuff she hadn't thought to collect before she left Sunnyside. It was only a matter of time before Morty took a dump on her floor, and yet she couldn't get motivated to get up.

"What the hell did I do to my career, Morty?" she asked when he came over and rubbed his torso along her arm. "I meant well... does that count for anything?"

He meowed, then disappeared under the bed to chase dust bunnies. Lauren's purse, dropped on top of the mattress when she first got home, started to vibrate and she dug out her phone.

"Hello?"

"Hey, it's Angelique, sorry I missed you on the way out," she said. "Gary's gone... what an asshole! I can't believe he fired you."

"Thank you... I kinda had it coming, though."

"What? No, you're the best director I've ever worked for," she said. "All you ever did was put our residents first."

"And my job second," Lauren said.

"Well, everybody misses you and Morty already," Angelique said. "It's gonna be really hard to find someone who can fill your shoes."

"How's Rose?" Lauren asked. "Has anyone heard?"

"Not yet," Angelique said. "Her lung sounds were decreased when I was examining her. If I had to guess, I'd say she's got pneumonia – fairly common in advanced stages of cancer."

"What's the outlook?"

"I don't know... with her age, it could go either way."

"Shit."

"Yeah." They both let the line go silent for a moment, reflecting on the massive shitstorm that today had turned out to be. Then Angelique asked, "Are you gonna keep Morty?"

"He's not going back to the shelter, that's for sure," Lauren answered. "I've never had a pet because I didn't have time for one... but I guess I have all sorts of time now."

"I'm here til eight tonight, but do you want me to come by with his toys and things after work?" Angelique offered.

"That would be great, actually," Lauren said. "You don't mind?"

"Anything for Morty," Angelique said. "And you too, I guess."

Lauren laughed. "Thanks."

They hung up, and Lauren called Grace. When she answered, the worry was immediately evident in her voice, in a single word. "Babe?"

"Hey."

"What's going on?"

Where to start? "Rose is in the hospital – Angelique thinks it's pneumonia, but I haven't heard anything official. And I'm unlikely to get any more updates, because Gary fired my ass."

"That bastard."

"Honestly, he had every right to," Lauren said. "What's worse is that he made me bring Morty with me – you should have seen how sad and confused everyone looked when I carried him out of there. I never should have got them a pet in the first place. I just made a huge mess of things."

"No, I'm the one who made the mess," Grace said. "Starting when I brought Sonic in. I'm sorry I got you fired."

Suddenly, the guilt and sadness that Lauren had been wallowing in switched to anger. It came over her so fast it took her breath away. "Actually, I'm only sorry that I worked for an asshole who cares so little for the people he's supposed to be serving. I'm sorry the Sunnyside residents got the short end of the stick in all this. I'm sorry Gary is such a short-sighted, scared little man."

"Me too," Grace answered. She gave a small laugh. "So, are you a Sphynx cat owner now?"

"I guess I am," Lauren said, and smiled. "I'm just glad he never predicted a resident's death like those creepy cats they write articles about. I'm not sure I could let him stay in my house if he had that power."

Grace laughed again. "Guess the name didn't quite fit after all. Can I come over? Bring some booze to cheer you up, maybe?"

"That'd be wonderful," Lauren said. "Oh shit!"

"What?"

"Literal shit, as in the one Morty just took in the corner," Lauren said. "I don't think I can wait on Angelique to bring a litter box."

"I'll stop at a pet store on my way over," Grace promised. "See you soon."

"Can't wait," Lauren said, and she hung up the phone smiling. Grace was the reason all of this happened, and she was also the reason Lauren was grinning. The reason her chest swelled at the thought of seeing her. The reason she was feeling optimistic all of a sudden, instead of depressed just an hour after she'd been fired.

Grace was a hell of a woman, and Lauren was pretty sure she loved her.

24
DEE

Sitting in a hospital waiting room all alone, wondering what was happening to the woman she loved was one of the worst feelings Dee had ever experienced. She'd been there for hours, although it felt like days, with no updates and no clue what was going on in the treatment room down the hall.

She was tired and hungry and she'd run out of comfortable positions that didn't make her hip ache, but none of that mattered when she remembered the sight of Rose lying unconscious on the hallway floor.

The only thing worse than this would be playing the exact same interminable waiting game back at Sunnyside, with no hope of hearing an update.

Gina had let Dee ride with Rose in the ambulance. That fact made Dee's head spin and she couldn't figure out what the hell had gotten into her, but she wasn't going to look a gift horse in the mouth. She just hopped into the ambulance – well, one of the paramedics hauled her into it – and was grateful that she got to hold Rose's hand on the way to the hospital.

She'd been conscious, with an oxygen mask preventing her from talking, and the medics said something to each other about fluid in her lungs. Dee's area of expertise was environmental science, not medicine, and she had no idea what that meant besides *not good.*

When they got to the hospital, Gina and Mike met them as the medics were unloading the stretcher. Gina must have driven through a rip in the time-space continuum in order to pick up her brother and still meet them outside the ER, but she'd managed, and her good will had run out by then.

"Wait in the lobby," she told Dee with a crispness that made her shiver. "I'll send someone out to update you when we know something."

Then Rose and the paramedics and Gina and Mike disappeared down the hall, and the paramedics came back a few minutes later with an empty stretcher. They left, and Dee took a seat. That was three hours ago, and either the doctors still didn't know what was wrong, or more likely, Gina had forgotten Dee even existed. Conveniently or otherwise.

She'd gone to the nurses' station a couple of times to inquire, but the ER was busy and she wasn't *really* family, so filling her in was low on the priority list.

So, Dee sat and waited as patiently as she could. She took out her phone and engaged in a bit of what the kids called 'doom scrolling' – looking up every complication for end-stage ovarian cancer she could find and trying to figure out the prognosis for each. With the one fact she did know – that Rose had fluid in her lungs – it didn't look optimistic, but she just kept scrolling, looking for some WebMD or American Cancer Society page that would tell her, 'Actually, this is good news! She's probably going to go into remission and outlive you.'

A woman could dream.

Angelique called at one point, to check on both Dee and Rose and ask her if she needed a ride back from the hospital. Oh, right. She hadn't given that a thought as she got into the ambulance, and the idea of asking Gina for a ride was good for a laugh. Dee said she would need one eventually, but she wasn't willing to leave yet – not until she'd heard something, one way or the other.

Angelique sounded off – like she was holding something back – but she didn't offer anything up and Dee was in no mood to press.

The other surprise while Dee sat there waiting was a text from Opal. She didn't even know Opal had her number, let alone that she cared enough to check in on her – especially after all the times Dee snapped at her.

The text itself was quintessentially Opal, packed to the brim with seemingly irrelevant emojis, along with the bizarre message, *Hope old Rosie is convalescing. Mr. Mortimer P. Sphynxkat was kidnapped at 1500 hours so we're gonna need every soldier Sunnyside's got to recover him!*

"Someone kidnapped..." Dee pinched the bridge of her nose, trying to decipher the message. "Okay, Opal."

She was still puzzling over that nonsensical text like

something out of one of the TV shows Opal liked to quote, when someone spoke her name.

"Dee?" It was so soft and gentle, and coming from Gina's mouth, that Dee's stomach immediately felt like it'd filled with rocks. There was no way this could be good news, but she rose from her seat anyway, trying to hold onto hope.

"Yes?"

"They've taken her for a lung biopsy," Gina said, coming and sitting beside Dee, leaving one chair between them. "Mike's got a migraine so he went looking for coffee. I told him to get you one."

Dee sat down before she fell down. The news about Rose was bad, but the fact that Gina actually thought of her at all? Shocking. "Thank you." She studied Gina for a moment, but didn't see any of the usual hostility in her eyes or her posture. So she decided to risk pushing the envelope. "So, what does that mean? The biopsy?"

"They want to know if the cancer has spread to her lungs," Gina said. "She definitely has pneumonia – she's been hiding her discomfort and fatigue from me because she didn't want me to worry. The fluid could be because of that, or it could be a sign that–"

Her voice cracked and she broke off. She put a hand to her mouth and Dee got the chance to study her for the first time since the day Gina slammed a door in her face. This was her adversary, yes, the woman who was trying to shut Rose up in her room and deny her a relationship almost sixty years in the making. But it was also a woman who had already lost one parent and was terrified of losing another.

Dee reached across the empty chair and put her hand on top of Gina's. The fact that she didn't immediately wrench it away was promising.

"I'm so sorry that you're going through this," Dee said. "Your mother is a wonderful woman and I've only known her a cumulative five months, but she's the most important person in my life." Gina listened silently, for once not shutting Dee down, so she kept talking. "I was never terribly close to my own parents so when I lost them it hurt, but it was nothing compared to how you will feel when Rose goes. I'm sorry you have to experience that."

"My father died ten years ago," Gina offered. "It was sudden – a massive heart attack that took him before the ambulance even arrived. It was nothing like this, watching my mother die slowly over years thanks to this fucking cancer."

"No matter how you lose a parent, it's awful."

"She got sick a year after he died, did you know that?" Gina asked. Dee shook her head. "To the day. She got her diagnosis on the one-year anniversary of his death, how unlikely is that?"

Dee didn't know what to say, so she just nodded and patted Gina's hand, surprised the woman was still allowing Dee to comfort her.

"The last ten years have been nothing but death and hospitals and enough meds to kill a horse, and the whole time I've had this invisible sword hanging over my head, waiting for a day like today, when I'd find out that she's finally losing the battle."

"Don't count her out just yet," Dee said, even though she knew fuck-all about Rose's condition or what her prospects were like. "She's cute and sweet, but underneath that, she's tough as hell."

Gina smiled. "She is. Do you love my mother?"

The question surprised Dee, but she didn't hesitate in her answer. "Since the first moment I laid eyes on her."

"I'm not a bigot, you know. It's not that."

"It's that you think your mother loving me means she loved your father less than you thought," Dee provided, and Gina nodded. "It's not true, though. In the last few months she's told me about your father, your family, her life after I knew her. And it's obvious how much she loves all three of you. Just because he's gone and I'm here doesn't invalidate that relationship."

Gina sniffed, and Dee realized she was crying. The woman who'd been the bane of her existence lately flipped her hand over and squeezed Dee's. "I know that now. It hurt to see her so obviously in love with you, even at a glance, and I had so many other feelings I wasn't dealing with... am still not dealing with. I reacted poorly."

"It's okay."

"It's not," Gina said. "For my mother's sake, if for no other reason. I want her to be happy and comfortable – that's why I moved her to Sunnyside in the first place. And if she's happy with you... then I'm happy."

"Thank you." Dee squeezed back, then found a tissue box on a nearby side table and offered it to Gina. She was blowing her nose when her brother appeared with a drink caddy full of coffees.

He passed them out, along with individual cream and sugar packets, then said, "I'm gonna guzzle this, then lie down in Mom's bed until she gets back, see if the caffeine helps. You okay here?"

"Yeah."

He looked at Dee. "You're Mom's friend from the home?"

Dee looked to Gina, unsure how much to say. "Yes–"

"This is Dee," Gina said. "The one Mom was in the Galapagos with."

"Oh wow," Mike said, recognition crossing his features. "Crazy you're here now."

"It really is," Dee agreed.

"She always talked like she missed you, when she mentioned that time in her life. I'm glad she has you now," he said, then turned and headed back up the hallway. His words didn't seem weighted with nearly the same meaning as when Dee spoke to Gina – he must not have picked up on all the details of their relationship.

But when Gina turned to Dee and said, "I'm glad too," her heart swelled with the acceptance she'd been hoping for all this time.

"Me three," she answered. Now, she just had to pray Rose had some fight left in her.

25
GRACE

When Lauren opened her front door, she had Mortimer wrapped around her neck like a stole. Her eyes lit up when she saw the armfuls of things Grace brought with her.

"What's all this?"

"Booze and a litter box, as promised," Grace said, "along with a tub of double fudge ice cream in case you feel like wallowing about the job, and a dozen roses because I'm sorry as hell for my part in you getting fired. And a bag of catnip for Morty in case he needs to take the edge off too. Although he looks pretty comfy."

"Yeah, I honestly never thought of myself as a cat person – or a pet person in general, really – but he climbed me like a tree fifteen minutes ago and he's literally growing on me," Lauren laughed as she helped Grace into the house with her things.

"Cats have a way of doing that," Grace agreed. "Me too, I hope."

Lauren took the bags out of Grace's hands, setting them on the floor just inside the door, and pulled her into a fierce kiss. Morty didn't seem bothered in the least and didn't move an inch.

"You definitely do," Lauren said. "I wouldn't mind if you climbed me like a tree a bit later."

"Oh yeah?"

"But first, litter box. I'd prefer it if there were no more accidents."

"Of course."

Grace followed Lauren and Morty into the spare bedroom, which Lauren explained was going to be her new hairless roommate's space. Grace unpacked the litter box and set it up, and while they worked, Lauren caught Grace up on everything that happened that day.

"It was probably the most eventful day of my life," Lauren said. "Most of it bad."

"Not all?"

"Well, this moment's not so bad."

Grace laughed. "You're filling up a litter box right now."

"Yeah, but I'm doing it with you."

The minute the lid was on the box, Morty hopped inside to make use of his new toilet. Apparently he'd been holding it politely for some time, and Grace and Lauren left the room to give him his privacy.

"I think we should head back out to the cabin soon," Grace said. "Get some much-needed R and R before whatever comes next for you."

"That sounds lovely," Lauren agreed. "Do you think

Morty will tolerate a long car ride? We can't leave him here for a whole weekend."

"He's pretty calm," Grace pointed out. "He didn't seem too bothered by the trip from the humane society to Sunnyside, and he looks comfortable here already." She slung her arm around Lauren's shoulders, pulling her into a hug. "You're putting on a brave face, but I know today was rough. I'm sorry you lost your job."

"Thank you."

"Are you gonna fight it? Sounds like everybody there will be lost without you."

"I don't see how I can," Lauren answered. "Gary had me dead to rights. I disobeyed him, and company policy."

"Ah, fuck company policy," Grace said. "All it does is keep good people from doing their jobs well."

"Sometimes," Lauren agreed. "Sometimes it keeps Opal from knocking a hole in her wall to make herself a double-wide suite."

Grace snorted. "Did she seriously try that?"

"Thankfully no, I don't think she has the upper body strength to wield a sledgehammer," Lauren answered. "But she did threaten it once, when the suite beside hers was unoccupied."

"Well, let's crack open the bottle of wine I brought – or the ice cream if you prefer, or both – and just chill for the rest of the night," Grace said. "We can work on world domination again tomorrow."

"That sounds perfect," Lauren said. "And this is definitely a 'both' kind of night, although I must admit I'm feeling much better since you got here."

Grace retrieved the ice cream and wine, and grabbed the catnip when she spotted Morty emerging from the spare bedroom to see what they were up to. Lauren went into the kitchen to find wine glasses, a corkscrew and big ice cream spoons, then met her on the couch.

They curled up together and Lauren asked, "So, what kind of wine goes with double fudge ice cream?"

"A dessert wine, of course," Grace answered. "I went with a Zin. Is it too nerdy to admit I actually googled it while I was standing in the wine department?"

"I love that you went to the trouble."

Lauren reached for the bag of catnip, and as soon as it was open, Morty started circling the floor in front of the couch like a shark. She sprinkled some of it on the shag rug beneath her coffee table, and he pounced on it with gusto. Lauren sat back, and Grace handed her a wine glass.

"To new opportunities," she suggested.

"New opportunities," Lauren agreed. "And better days ahead – together."

They kissed, then drank. Grace told Lauren about taking Snow to get his ear patched up, and how all the people involved seemed more traumatized than he did.

"Do you think there's any chance in hell that the puppy playtimes will continue now that you're not at Sunnyside?" she wondered.

"Not if Gary has anything to say about it," Lauren grumbled. "Maybe we were going about it wrong, though. Maybe instead of bringing the dogs to the residents, we should have tried it the other way around. That could still work."

"Not all of them would be able to go though, right?" Grace asked with a frown. "Rose, if she's not feeling up to it. Cora has her bad days, too."

"Yeah, that was the beauty of bringing the puppies to them," Lauren agreed. "But I guess an imperfect solution is still better than nothing at all. Angelique's coming over to drop off Morty's things after her shift – maybe we can run it by her and see what she thinks."

"When's she getting here?" Grace asked.

"A little after eight."

Grace checked her watch. "It's five now. I have something I'd like to run by you in the meantime... or over you. My hands, my body, my tongue."

She pounced like Morty on his catnip. Set the wine glasses aside and let the ice cream melt in its tub. Laid Lauren down on the couch and kissed her senseless. She could taste the sweet wine on Lauren's tongue, and desire pulsed through her, unleashed like a tide surging over the breakers after a long and trying day.

"I need you," she breathed against Lauren's lips.

"I love you," Lauren answered, her hands cupping Grace's cheeks, holding her close.

"You do?" Grace's eyes popped open, gazing into the deep chocolate of Lauren's eyes.

"Yes," she said. "I do."

"I love you too. Fuck, I love you so much."

"Then take me," Lauren said. "Make love to me, Grace."

She got up, and Lauren frowned.

"Where are you going?" she asked. "Leaving is the opposite of what I just–"

Before she could finish her sentence, Grace grabbed her by the hand and hauled her to her feet. "I can't do this in front of Morty – it'd traumatize him," she explained. Then she practically dragged Lauren down the hall to her bedroom, stopping to press her up against the wall for a kiss here, yank her shirt over her head there.

She kicked the door shut when they got to their destination, and made quick work of stripping Lauren the rest of the way bare.

"God, you're the most gorgeous woman I've ever laid eyes on." She dropped to her knees to kiss Lauren's belly, squeeze her supple hips, glide her hands over her round ass. Then she nestled her face between Lauren's legs and planted a soft kiss on her clit. "And this is my favorite place in the world to be. Lie down."

Lauren obliged, but slowly. She sauntered over to the bed, letting Grace watch her hips sway. Then she turned around, sat down, and spread her thighs – all while giving Grace the most delicious *fuck me* eyes she'd ever seen.

Grace followed her, stripping off her own layers as she went. She bent down and kissed Lauren, just long enough to tease her, then put her hands on Lauren's shoulders and shoved her down onto her back. Then Grace dropped to her knees before her.

She licked Lauren nice and slow, just as teasingly as Lauren had walked across the room earlier. Lauren reached down and closed her fingers in Grace's short hair, letting her know she was hitting just the right spot.

"That feels so good," she said, her thighs quaking against Grace's cheeks in confirmation.

"Yeah?" Grace paused to torture her further. "How about this?"

She slipped one finger into Lauren's slick sex, then another.

"Oh God." Lauren's hand tightened in Grace's hair, so much that it hurt – in a way she wanted more of. Grace grinned then brought her mouth back down to lap at Lauren's sweet pussy. This was better than wine and ice cream – better by far.

She had her coming just a moment later – faster than Grace wanted, honestly, she would have been happy to continue teasing Lauren for quite a bit longer. But they had all night, and after that, the rest of their lives. There would be plenty of time for long, languid orgasms in the future.

When she felt Lauren clamp around her fingers, Grace took the cue and started fucking her harder, sending her to new heights as Lauren screamed and switched to clutching the bedsheets like she might float away if she didn't hold on.

26
LAUREN

They lost track of time, and when the doorbell rang in what felt like the middle of the night, Lauren shot upright in bed, out of Grace's arms.

"Oh shit, I forgot about Angelique. And I'm naked."

Grace laughed. "I'm sure she'll wait."

"She just got off a long shift, I don't want to make her stand on my porch while I get dressed..." Lauren was casting about for her clothes, which she'd lost partially in the bedroom, and also partly in the hallway.

"Here," Grace said, handing her panties to her. "You get dressed, I'll throw on a robe and let her in, okay?"

"Thanks," Lauren said. "Make sure Morty doesn't get out – I don't know yet how much of an escape artist he is, but judging by the incident with Snow, he is a troublemaker."

"I won't," Grace promised.

Lauren took a split second to admire the way Grace looked in her bathrobe – a plush pink thing that was definitely more feminine than Grace's usual wardrobe. The juxtaposition was certainly appealing. Then she turned her attention back to finding her clothes.

A minute or two later, she went into the living room to find Grace helping Angelique with several banker boxes full of Morty's things.

"Wow, he accumulated all that already?" Lauren asked. Morty roused from his catnip haze to come over and sniff at everything.

"There are a lot of people at Sunnyside who love him," Angelique said, but there was a pall over her expression.

"What?" Lauren asked. Was she still upset about Lauren getting fired?

"I don't know if you're gonna want to hear this..."

"Well, now you have to tell us," Grace said.

"I found the rat," Angelique said.

"The rat?" Grace asked, but Lauren understood.

"The person who's been telling Gary about all the animal programs," she explained, then turned to Angelique. "You're right, I'm not sure I want to know... not a member of the staff, is it?"

Angelique shook her head.

"Gina?" Lauren guessed. That woman had enough spite to fill three people and it wouldn't have surprised her if she found out Gina was tattling on her simply because the rules were being broken.

"Nope," Angelique said, then sighed. "Opal."

Lauren and Grace's jaws both dropped.

"*Opal?* She loves the animals!" Lauren objected. "Why would she do that?"

"Turns out Gary had a few more tricks up his sleeve than we realized," Angelique said. "He's been texting her, pretending to conduct surveys about Sunnyside. And you know how Opal loves to talk."

"That sneaky asshole," Lauren said. "She's the perfect person to get dirt from – give her the slightest bit of attention and she'll put on a whole show."

Angelique nodded. "Don't be mad at her, please."

"No, I'm not," Lauren said. "Gary, on the other hand..."

Angelique sighed again. "There's more."

"More?"

"He hung around for a while in the afternoon," Angelique said. "I figured he was securing your computer or writing up an incident report or something. But after you and I spoke on the phone, he called me into your office."

"My old office," Lauren corrected.

"Well..." Angelique hesitated, biting her lower lip. She'd never been so timid and it piqued Lauren's interest, but also made her nervous.

"What?"

"He offered me your job."

"Oh shit," Grace said, looking from Angelique to Lauren as if steam were about to start coming out of her ears.

"Are you mad?" Angelique asked.

Lauren's brow furrowed. "What? No. Are you going to take it?"

"You're seriously not mad?" Angelique pressed.

"Why would I be?"

"Because you got fired and I got offered a promotion to take your job in the space of a couple of hours?" Angelique pointed out.

"I'm not mad," Lauren assured her. "Getting fired is no fun, but neither is working for Gary – you should know that before you accept the position. Unless you already have?"

"No, I wanted to talk to you first."

Lauren cracked a smile. "Well, you did say just a couple hours ago that my shoes will be hard to fill. I guess you're gonna get first-hand experience with that."

"So you think I should take it?"

"I think somebody who truly cares about the residents should be the facility director," Lauren said. "And you have always put them first. You're even good with Opal. If you want it, take it. And don't let Gary steamroll you."

Angelique laughed. "We'll touch base in six months and see if I've been fired too." She yawned and checked the time on her watch. "It's getting late and I have an opening shift tomorrow. I better get going."

"Thanks for bringing Morty his things," Lauren said. The three of them moved toward the door and Lauren gave Angelique a hug. "Good luck, and call me if you need any advice, or want to vent about Gary. Don't be a stranger."

"I won't," Angelique promised. "Hey, what are you gonna do?"

"I don't know, but I'll be okay," Lauren said.

Grace took her hand, and they watched Angelique walk down the sidewalk to her car. Then Grace turned to Lauren. "You really okay with all that?"

"Yeah, if I got to hire my replacement, I would have picked her," Lauren said. "The Opal thing though... wow."

"Yeah, that Gary is a real turd." They went back over to the couch, and Grace picked up the carton of ice cream still sitting on the coffee table. "Want some ice cream soup?"

Lauren laughed. "Nah, I'll pass. Refreeze it and we can have it later... when we need to cool down."

She gave Grace a wink, then pounced on her again.

27
DEE

Dee got to see Rose after she got back from her biopsy. She was sedated, so Dee simply sat by her bedside and held her hand, sending every ounce of healing energy she could muster into Rose. She'd never been a praying type, or really spiritual at all. She was a scientist and she had faith in facts, in numbers. In plans.

Her only plan right now was to hope as hard as she possibly could. And it felt rotten, but it was all she had to hold onto.

Gina and Mike let Dee be in the room alone with Rose for a while, but eventually a nurse came to say that visiting hours were long gone, and they'd already bent the rules to let them all stay as long as they had.

Dee got to her feet, then leaned over the bed to kiss Rose's cheek. "Don't you leave me now, you hear?"

She went out to the lobby, clueless about what time it was, wondering if there would even be enough staff working the overnight shift at Sunnyside to spare someone to come pick her up. She might be learning the ins and outs of rideshares at the ripe old age of eighty-two.

But then Gina surprised her. "Come on, I'll take you home."

"Really? You don't mind?"

"Well, somebody's got to," Gina said, but she gave a small smile.

"Thank you. And thanks for letting me see her."

"She would have wanted that if she'd been awake," Gina said. Then she kicked the bottom of her brother's shoe. He was stretched across three lobby chairs, his arm thrown over his eyes. "Mike, time to go."

"Mmmphh," he grunted, and slowly got to his feet. His migraine was obviously still raging, and between that and Dee's aching hip, it took them a while to make it outside.

Gina jogged ahead to bring the car around, and while Dee stood alone with Mike, enjoying the cool night air, he asked, "So you were friends with my mom back in the day, and now you live together. What are the odds?"

"Astronomical," Dee smiled.

"Well, I like knowing she has a friend at that place," he said. "I'm not great with all this *hospitals and cancer and nursing homes* stuff. As you can probably tell."

"Everyone grieves differently," Dee said. She put her hand on Mike's shoulder. "But I hope we have a good long time left with your mother."

When Gina arrived with the car, Mike lay down in the backseat and Gina helped Dee into the front passenger seat. None of them were in a talking mood, and the silence and the gentle movement of the car brought forward a bone-deep exhaustion that Dee had been trying to suppress all day. She rested her head against the window, eyes fluttering shut, and didn't even realize she'd fallen asleep until Gina nudged her awake.

"We're here," she said, uncharacteristically softly. "Mike, help Dee into the building – it's the least you can do since you've been useless all day."

At least I'm not the only one she harangues, Dee thought as Mike opened her door and held out his hand. Before she took it, she turned to Gina. "Will you please keep me informed about Rose?"

Gina nodded, and Dee let Mike haul her out of the car like a sack of potatoes. They got to the door, where a caregiver was waiting with a wheelchair. He pushed Dee down the unusually silent halls and past Rose's empty room. If she had to guess, she would have said that this would be a sleepless night, but age and fatigue won out and she was asleep again the minute she was in her bed.

Rose stayed in the hospital for nearly a week. Her biopsy results came back the next day – negative for lung cancer, thankfully. She did have pleural effusion and pneumonia, which weren't uncommon for someone of her age and health status, but still very serious, especially since she'd been downplaying her symptoms for a time.

Dee wasn't able to get anyone to take her to the hospital again. Sunnyside was understaffed and chaotic after Lauren was fired – Dee was upset about that, but her mind was almost entirely on Rose so she hadn't taken the time to process the news and think about how Lauren must be feeling. And she couldn't bring herself to ask Gina to make extra trips to Sunnyside just to drive her back and forth, even if they had reached somewhat of an understanding with each other. At least she was keeping Dee in the loop about Rose's condition.

Which was improving. Slowly but surely.

Don't you leave me, Dee had told her, and whether or not Rose heard it, she was granting Dee's request – or rather, demand.

She was on medication, and receiving oxygen therapy. And according to Gina's brief daily updates, she was getting better and stronger each day. On Tuesday, nearly a week after Rose was admitted, Gina left Dee one of the best voicemails she'd ever heard.

"The doctor says my mother's lungs are clear enough for her to be released," she said. Of course she'd called while Dee was in the shower, so she couldn't ask any questions. "It'll likely be tomorrow, maybe not until the afternoon because of how slow these things move. My mother's been asking about you... she'd like to see you when she gets home."

Dee's heart was soaring by the end of that short message. There was no more talk of Gina's power of attorney, and it sounded like that ugly period was well and truly behind them. And Rose was coming back to her!

She got dressed as fast as she could and went out to the hallway, where she found Angelique at the nurses' station. She'd been promoted to Lauren's old job, but until she found a replacement for her among the nursing staff, she was pulling double duty. At least she was doing it with a smile on her face.

"Hey, Dee, how are you today?" she asked as Dee came to lean on the counter.

"Fantastic – Rose is coming home tomorrow."

"Oh, wonderful," Angelique said. "I'll have to find out what her favorite meal is and make sure we serve it for dinner for her."

"Potato pancakes," Dee said. "At least that was her favorite back on Santa Cruz Island. Her palate may have changed since then."

"That's perfect," Angelique said, making a quick note on a Post-it. "Breakfast for dinner with potato pancakes to welcome Rose home."

"Actually, I had another idea," Dee said. "I know you're really busy..."

"What is it?"

Dee explained the perfect welcome-home gift that had come to her the minute she heard Rose was coming back, as if planted in her head through divine inspiration. Angelique said she loved it, but frowned.

"It sounds like a tall order for such a small amount of time," she said. "And we're short staffed."

"I know," Dee said. "But I figured I'd ask – if anyone could pull it off, it'd be you… or Lauren."

Angelique brightened. "That's it! I'll call Lauren and see if she's available to help."

"You think she'd mind?"

"I think she'd love to be included," Angelique said. "Look at how much trouble she and Grace went to so you and Rose could go to the zoo."

"Would you give me her number?" Dee asked. "I'd like to ask her myself."

Angelique wrote it down on another Post-it, and Dee took it out to her favorite outdoor spot on the patio. She called Lauren and explained her idea, and Lauren said that she'd be happy to help.

"I've been getting some R and R this week, per the doctor's orders," she said, then chuckled. "Dr. Grace, that is. Next week, I get back out there and start looking for jobs, but for the rest of the day, I'm at your disposal. And I think this will be a lovely gesture."

And that was how, the following day after lunch, Dee ended up with a string of turtles for the tortoise-obsessed love of her life.

Lauren brought Grace with her when she dropped off the plant, and Dee was delighted to see that it was potted in a ceramic planter that looked just like the giant tortoises Rose used to study. The plant itself was a succulent made up of small, perfectly round leaves with a variegated pattern like that on a turtle's shell.

"It's even better than I expected!" Dee exclaimed when she saw it. "How did you find that planter?"

"That's what took so long," Lauren explained. "We got the string of turtles at the first garden center we went to, but it was in a pretty boring hanging basket. I thought something like this would be better."

"She dragged me around to every nursery in the city," Grace explained. "But I have to hand it to her, the end result is pretty good."

"It's perfect," Dee said. "Thank you so much."

"We're just happy you and Rose get your happy-ever-after," Lauren said, and Grace tucked her arm around Lauren's waist.

"Looks like you two are headed that way too," Dee said. "Hold onto each other – love is the most important thing in the world. I spent most of my life telling myself that wasn't true, only because my love had come and gone. But now that I have her back... she's all I want and all I need in this world."

"That and a string of turtles," Grace smiled.

"You want to stick around for a while?" Dee asked. "I don't know exactly when she's getting here, but we're having a special dinner for her."

Lauren shook her head. "Grace invited the owner of Granville Estates over for dinner – she might have an opening for me when her current director retires in a few months. We need to go home and cook her a 'please hire me' pot roast."

"She'd be a fool not to," Dee said. "And if you need me to go on record with that, I'd be happy to."

Lauren and Grace left, and Dee borrowed a wheelchair, setting the string of turtles on it and pushing it up the hall to Rose's suite. She set it on the dining table, where Rose would be able to see it from her recliner and it would have plenty of sunlight from the big window. She was still fussing over it, arranging the delicate strings, when she heard footsteps behind her, and the squeak of rubber on the waxed floor.

Dee turned, and smiled from ear to ear when she saw Rose in the doorway. She was sitting in a wheelchair and she had an oxygen cannula under her nose, but she'd never looked more beautiful.

"You're home," Dee said, crossing the floor to her.

Rose stood, Gina trying and failing to keep her in her chair, but for once, Rose brushed her daughter off. "Give me a minute, please, honey."

Gina reluctantly obeyed, though she gave Dee an approving nod before she disappeared into the hallway. Dee put her arms around Rose. "I missed you so much. I was scared you were leaving me."

"I'm not going anywhere," Rose said. "At least not without you."

Dee couldn't help laughing. "Is that a threat?"

Rose shook her head. "It's a promise. It may have taken me sixty years, but I'm ready to be yours, all yours, and I don't care who knows it. I told Gina as much on the ride over. They're going to have to pry us apart."

"I won't let them," Dee answered.

"Neither will I. Now kiss me, damn it."

Dee grinned, and lowered her lips to Rose's. They had a lot of lost time to make up for, and there was nothing she'd rather do.

28

ROSE

1964

It was late by research station standards – once it got dark out, people tended to retire to their barracks or play cards in the cafeteria until bedtime. It was an early to bed, early to rise kind of place, and ordinarily that suited Rose just fine. The tortoises followed the same schedule, after all.

Tonight, though, she had other plans.

She'd eaten dinner with Dee and their usual group – mostly the other women in camp, and Peter hung around at times too, drawn to the estrogen like a moth to a flame, oblivious to the fact that most of the aforementioned flames were entirely disinterested in him. It turned out he wasn't bad company, though – especially when the talk turned to science. He acted cocky and obnoxious, but when it came right down to the work, Peter wasn't entirely useless. Who knew?

The group's normal evening activities involved

playing Hearts or drinking beer and swapping stories from their lives back home to entertain each other. On this particular night, Rose swiped a discreet hand along Dee's lower back and said, "Frank wasn't acting right earlier today – I promised my supervisor I'd check in on him before bed. See you in the barracks."

"Okay... tell Frank I hope he feels better," Dee said.

Rose smiled. Dee had come to love the tortoises almost as much as Rose did, and came by to help feed them breakfast whenever she could spare the time. Of course, there was nothing wrong with Frank today, but Dee would find that out soon enough.

It was a little unnerving walking through the jungle with nothing but a flashlight and a backpack in the dark, but Rose made her way to the tortoise enclosure and started getting ready by the moonlight. By the time Dee arrived about thirty minutes later, holding up the note Rose had left in her bunk directing her there, Rose had set up the space the same way Dee had arranged her office the first time they were alone together.

The tortoises were asleep in the covered part of their enclosure, and Rose had laid a blanket out in an open area on the other side of the fence. A couple of beers and two servings of tonight's dessert from the cafeteria – strawberry shortcake – were waiting for them on the blanket.

"How's Frank?" Dee asked with a knowing smirk, stepping up to Rose.

"Fine and dandy," Rose said. "I don't think he'll mind

being used as a puppet in my plan. Do you like the surprise?"

"I love it," Dee said, coming closer. She kicked off her shoes and stepped onto the blanket, pulling Rose against her. "I think our fellow scientists would be aghast to know what we do after hours, though."

"I'm pretty sure at least two of the other girls have made the unfortunate choice to sleep with Peter," Rose pointed out. "They can't judge."

Dee scooped Rose into her arms, eliciting a girly squeal from Rose that was very much unlike her – or at least, unlike the woman she thought she was before she'd met Dee. When she was with Dee, things were different. Better. *Right.*

She'd awakened Rose in so many ways, to possibilities and feelings she had no idea even existed. And she wanted Rose to be just as free and open as she was.

Rose bit her bottom lip, looking up through her lashes at Dee in a glance she'd learned was sure to drive her wild. "Make love to me," she said. Then, her grin widening, she added, "Fuck me senseless."

"I like the sound of that." Dee laid her down on the blanket, the firm, corded muscles of her shoulders appearing in the moonlight as she shrugged off her button-up shirt.

"You're gorgeous," Rose said, feeling breathless and dizzy as she drank Dee in.

"So are you," Dee answered. "The most beautiful woman I've ever seen. I love you."

I love you too.

Rose lay on her back, watching Dee methodically strip off every layer before she started on Rose's clothes, working her way up from her pants to her shirt. They hadn't touched the beers, and yet Rose felt like she might float away at any moment – if Dee weren't here holding her, keeping her right here on earth.

"I wish I could freeze this moment."

A brief sadness washed over her as thoughts of the real world threatened to worm their way in. Home. Grad school. The parade of men her mother wanted to set her up with. Life beyond the Galapagos, which couldn't possibly be as good as this.

"We can," Dee promised.

"How?"

"Close your eyes," she instructed.

Rose did as she was told. For a moment, nothing happened. It stretched out for so long that she was tempted to open her eyes, lift her head and see what Dee was doing.

And then she felt her.

Fingertips trailing down her hips, over her curves. Breath warm and welcome between her thighs. Lips gently kissing Rose's most intimate place. And then Dee's mouth withdrew.

She spoke softly, teasing kisses over Rose's mons and down the inside of her thigh as she did so. "This right here is my heaven. You. Me. Nothing else exists when I'm with you, and time stands still every time I bury my face in your pretty little pussy."

And then she did just that.

Rose arched her back, fingers threading into Dee's short hair. She gasped and writhed beneath her, and Dee was right – time stood still even as her heart sped up, and for a brief and beautiful moment, everything was perfect.

EPILOGUE—LAUREN

6 MONTHS LATER

Lauren stepped outside and drew a deep breath. Cold winter air bit at her lungs, but she didn't care – nothing could get her down today.

She'd just finished her interview at Granville Estates, where the current director would have a hand in hiring and training her replacement. She'd given Lauren a rave review when the facility owner asked what she thought, and they'd all but offered her the job right there on the spot.

"We have to go through all the proper channels," Lauren's almost-new-boss, Dion, said. "But you're our final interview and off the record, expect a call from us Monday morning."

She was beaming as she walked to her car, hugging her coat tight around her, and the minute she was inside it with the heat blasting, she dialed Grace.

"Babe?" her girlfriend's voice came over the car speaker, full of anticipation. "How did it go?"

"Great," Lauren said. "I really love the facility, and I got to meet a few of the residents as well."

"Did you meet Doris, a.k.a. Opal Two?" Grace asked with a laugh.

"Not yet," Lauren said. "There's always one, isn't there?"

"So you think you're gonna get it?"

A little ripple of anxiety worked its way into Lauren's chest and she decided not to jinx it by being too optimistic. "I think I have a good chance. I really want it."

"You're going to be amazing there," Grace said. "Come home and we'll get on the road."

They were going out to the cabin to celebrate, despite Lauren's objections that there was nothing to celebrate just yet.

"You're *gonna* get the job," Grace said. "They've been courting you for months!"

"I'm afraid to want it too bad," Lauren confessed. Granville Estates was everything she wanted out of an assisted-living facility, and they'd been working with Grace and her business for almost a year now. Best of all, no Gary – no corporate at all.

"I'll see you soon," Lauren said. "Love you."

"Love you too, babe, drive safe."

There was a light dusting of snow on the ground, the first one of the season, and that meant everyone was driving like they'd completely forgotten what all this cold white stuff was and how slippery it could be.

She drove cautiously, making her way to her little

bungalow, which in the past six months had become *her and Grace's* little bungalow. And Morty, of course.

Lauren had been applying for jobs, but Grace had encouraged her to take her time and find the *right* position, where she could make the most difference and where they wouldn't work her to death the way Sunnyside had. In the meantime, Lauren worked with Grace to grow Williams Animal-Assisted Therapy. It turned out she was a pretty good contact to have, what with all the medical professionals she knew, and Grace's business was thriving more than ever.

The Granville Estates job had been looming this whole time, and now it was as if all the pieces were finally falling into place. Everything about life was just perfect.

When she got home, Lauren parked her car in the garage and found Grace loading up her truck with supplies for the weekend. Morty was already in the cab, curled up on top of Grace's coat and wearing a fuzzy purple sweater. He didn't mind long car rides, and it turned out he was a bit of a predator after all, terrorizing the small rodents all around the cabin every time they drove down.

Lauren gave Grace a quick hug and promised to tell her all about the job interview during the drive, then started helping her load up the truck.

"Is that the sweater Anita sent him?" she asked as she set her bag in the footwell and gave Morty a quick scritch behind the ears.

"Yeah, she's getting pretty good at knitting," Grace said. "There's a big pink heart on his chest."

Lauren laughed. "Cheesy much?"

They hadn't been able to bring Mortimer back to Sunnyside for visits because Gary was still busy being his usual, terrible self, but Angelique did occasionally bring some of the residents by to visit – with Lauren and Grace as much as the Sphynx. They were all still attached to old Morty, as Opal called him, and last time they came, Angelique let slip the rumor that Gary was in hot water of his own.

"Corporate was none too happy when I told them about what he was doing texting Opal under false pretenses," she said with scandal in her eyes. "So he was already in trouble. Now I'm hearing through the grapevine that he's so obsessed with his numbers that he actually fudged them in his favor for the Youngstown location."

"I can't believe that," Lauren had said. "Actually, I can – that man would do anything to make his spreadsheets look neat and orderly."

"Well, I'd say he's not long for Sunnyside," Angelique went on, then turned to Grace. "So if you want to try to get the service dogs back in, which clearly the residents would love, we may have a new corporate overlord soon, one who may be friendlier about that stuff."

All that was still in the works, but Lauren and Grace had been on the edges of their seats waiting to hear about Gary's fate. The waiting would be pure torture for him too, which gave Lauren a certain amount of wicked satisfaction.

Angelique had been keeping them in the loop about

all that, and also about the two lovebirds she had on her hands. Rose made a full recovery, and it didn't take long for Gina to see just what a positive influence Dee was on her. She did a complete turnaround, and even showed up on moving day when Rose and Dee moved into a larger couples' suite together.

For the rest of today, though, Lauren only had eyes for Grace – and Morty, of course.

"I can't wait to get out to the cabin and light a fire and curl up with you in front of it," she said as the two of them finished packing and hopped into the truck.

"I'm gonna get you naked and keep you that way all weekend," Grace said, reaching over Morty to squeeze Lauren's thigh.

She started the truck and backed out of the garage, and Lauren noticed a pair of travel mugs in the cupholders. "I don't recognize those, did you buy new mugs?"

"Yeah, made us our first batch of hot chocolate for the season," Grace said. "Aren't they cute?"

Lauren narrowed her eyes. *Cute* was not the type of word that typically came out of Grace's mouth. "What are you up to?"

"Nothing," Grace shrugged, unconvincingly.

"Well, can I have my cocoa now?" Lauren asked. "Or do I have to wait?"

"Go ahead," Grace said. She was struggling not to grin, and Lauren couldn't help smiling along with her.

"What is going on with you over there?" she asked as she lifted her mug out of the cupholder.

"Absolutely nothing," Grace said.

The mug was ceramic, warm in Lauren's hands, with a knitted cozy wrapped around it that matched the color of Morty's sweater.

"Did Anita make this too?" she asked.

Grace finally nodded. "Yeah, I wanted to get you a little something to celebrate the new job."

"I haven't gotten it yet," Lauren pointed out.

"You will. And I want to make sure you continue to get plenty of R and R even while you're kicking ass as the best facility director in town," Grace said. "So these travel mugs will remind us to take time off at the cabin."

She lifted her own mug out of its cupholder and pulled off the cozy to reveal a message painted on the ceramic. There was a forest scene, just like the view from the cabin, and beneath it, the words, *Let the adventure begin.*

"Aww, that's cute," Lauren said. She pulled the cozy off her own mug, and her heart stopped for a moment. "Wait..."

Grace was beaming at her, barely even paying attention to the road anymore despite the snow.

"Is this for real?" Lauren asked.

Her mug had the same forest scene, but the message was different. It said, *Will you marry me?*

Grace started pulling the truck over to the side of the road, and Morty perked up, sensing a change in the energy between them. "I can't drive and do this."

"Do what?" Lauren asked. Her heartbeat was catching up to her, pounding in her chest now.

"Propose," Grace said. She parked on the side of the

road, then turned to Lauren. "I actually was planning to wait until we got to the cabin. I figured you'd have no reason to look under the cozy until I was ready for you to... but then I couldn't help myself."

"You want to marry me?" Lauren asked, still stunned.

"Of course," Grace said. "You're the most amazing woman I've ever met, and one thing I've learned over the last year is that when you find someone who makes your whole world brighter, you can't let them go. You have to let them know just how much you love and appreciate them every chance you get, and you have to savor every moment together."

Lauren's heart leaped into her throat when Grace lifted Morty up, revealing the big pink heart. What Grace failed to mention earlier was that it was not just decoration – it was a pocket. She reached inside and pulled out a small velvet pouch.

"Thanks for keeping this safe for me, Mort," she said, setting him back down on her coat. Then she opened the pouch and pulled out a delicate gold band studded with chocolate diamonds. "I hope you don't mind that they're not pure diamonds – these ones reminded me of your eyes."

"I love it," Lauren said. "I love you."

"Will you be my wife?"

It was a damn good thing Grace had pulled the car over, because Lauren lunged at her then.

Morty scurried onto the safety of the dashboard, and Lauren threw her arms around Grace, climbing into her lap even in the relatively small space of the truck cab. "I would love nothing more in the world than to be your wife. No matter what else happens in life, all I want is you – I'm up for any adventure with you by my side."

Grace kissed her then, and slid the ring onto Lauren's finger. "Let the adventure begin."

Read the rest of the Fur-Ever series

LESFIC BOOK CLUB

Calling all lesfic lovers!

Join us for a monthly book club discussion featuring your favorite sapphic fiction authors. Sign up for notifications when we pick a new book here: https://amzn.to/3JkaS5p

The discussion takes place on Slack - come say hello at www.lesficlove.com

Printed in Great Britain
by Amazon